# TWO SHOTS FOR THE SHERIFF

When Estevan Ramirez bursts, guns blazing, into a Silver City saloon, is it the signal for a range war between two rival cattle clans? Or can the whiskey-loving sheriff, Steve McCormack, subdue the bloodshed? His job is not helped by the fact that renegade Apaches and a crazed killer are on the loose. Steve bucks the booze, straddles his mule and hits the trail. Can he bring peace to this wildest corner of the old west?

JOHN DYSON

# TWO SHOTS FOR THE SHERIFF

*Complete and Unabridged*

## LINFORD
Leicester

First published in Great Britain in 2002 by
Robert Hale Limited
London

First Linford Edition
published 2003
by arrangement with
Robert Hale Limited
London

British Library CIP Data

Dyson, John, *1943 –*
    Two shots for the sheriff.—Large print ed.—
Linford western library
1. Western stories
2. Large type books
I. Title
823.9'14 [F]

ISBN 1–8439–5078–2

Published by
F. A. Thorpe (Publishing)
Anstey, Leicestershire

Set by Words & Graphics Ltd.
Anstey, Leicestershire
Printed and bound in Great Britain by
T. J. International Ltd., Padstow, Cornwall

# 1

The sun was sinking behind the ragged peaks in a blaze of glory, streaking the sky crimson and gold as Estevan stepped into the saloon. He stood silhouetted in the doorway in his tight leathers and wide-brimmed sombrero against a sky the colour of fire and blood. He had chosen his moment well.

The Kid blinked his eyes against the blaze of light. A chill went through him. There was something uncanny about the Mexican, like an avenger out of hell. He looked about him at the boys for support, but they were scraping away their chairs from around the card-table, moving fast out of the way of flying lead, making it clear this was none of their business. This was between Estevan Ramirez and the Kid.

For moments the Kid felt like a jack-rabbit transfixed in the path of a stoat. He swallowed his saliva, his heart thumping, his fingers fluttering over the buckhorn butt of his fifty-dollar double-action Smith & Wesson .44 calibre.

'You got a nerve coming here,' he said, hoarsely.

Through narrowed eyes Estevan glanced at the *Americano* cowpunchers and riff-raff who had fanned away along the bar. He did not know whether to expect trouble from them, or not. He did not care. He kept his stance, his hands spread-eagled over the twin, silver-enscrolled .38s double-slung low across his hips.

'I'm here for you, Kid. Get up off that chair. You owe me a thousand dollars. You haven't paid. My patience is at an end. Now you must pay the other way.'

'A cool thousand? You crazy?' The Kid tried to laugh but it came out more like a croaking gasp of pain. 'I was drunk, high on red-eye in that card-game. I hadn't a clue what I was doin'. You knew that. You took advantage. It was just a joke to me. You don't think I'd take a crooked game with some lousy greaser serious, do you? Get out of here 'fore you get hurt.'

'Enough of your insults,' Estevan shouted. 'Come on, draw.'

The Kid didn't bother getting to his feet, but pushed the table over as a shield, and, crouching low, jerked out his .44. His shot crashed out and cut the Mexican's high cheekbone. In reply, Estevan's revolver seemed to spring into his right fist. It spurted flame.

For seconds the saloon reverberated to a continuous cacophony of explosions as the Kid wildly fired his Smith & Wesson at the dark shape in the blazing doorway, and Estevan fanned the hammer of his Lightning.

'Aagh!' The Kid screamed as a slug thudded like a red-hot bolt across his wrist, sending his revolver spinning. The oak table was splintered by shots. He tried to scramble across the floor. Pain pierced his consciousness as another bullet slashed through his calf and cut him down.

'Get him!' he pleaded to the stern-faced watching men. 'Oh, God! My leg! Do something!'

'You want to try?' Estevan flipped out his left-hand Lightning and aimed its deathly hole at them. But, as none seemed ready to accept the invitation, the lips of his handsome, copper-skinned face curled in a sneer. 'No, I did not think so.'

The Kid had backed up to sit leaning against the bar, holding onto his leg, moaning. 'Don't shoot! Please! I'm too young to die. My old man, he'll pay you.'

'He better. If not,' Estevan sneered, 'next time I kill you. You tell him if I don't get my money I will take what I'm owed out of his herd.'

Black powder-smoke drifted as the slim Mexican stood for moments waiting, watching, but the men stood in silence like skulking wolves. Estevan was renowned as one of the deadliest shootists on the frontier.

'Remember what I say.' The Mexican backed out of the batwing doors into the dusty street. He glanced about him, but what few people were about in the stores and barber shop showed little interest. The blamming of six-guns was not unusual hereabouts. Best not to get involved.

The Mexican holstered his guns, stepped around a hitching rail and swung on to his blue-eyed grey. To the touch of his spurs and the jerk of the bridle the fine stallion spurted away in fiery fashion and went at a gallop along the main street, kicking up dirt, Estevan leaning low over his flying mane. 'Yaagh!' he shouted. 'Go!'

\* \* \*

Sheriff Steve McCormack tumbled out of his adobe office and jailhouse to see what the commotion was about. He had been aroused from a deep siesta induced by a bottle of rotgut and his mouth tasted like cotton wool.

5

'He's in a hurry, ain't he?' He recognized Estevan's mount going hell for leather across the plain in a curving trail heading south. 'What's he been up to?' The rider disappeared before McCormack could raise his rifle for a half-mile long-shot. All that was left was his drifting plume of dust.

'Shee-it! Can't a man have a peaceful siesta any more? Why are people allus causing me trouble? What's the matter with them? Why do they allus have to be shootin', robbin', cheatin', killin' and runnin'? In my opinion it's too durn hot.'

Steve ran fingers through his crop of blond hair and spat in the dust, addressing the remarks partly to a wizened storekeeper who had called across, 'What's happening, sheriff?' and partly to his wolfhound, Jock. He wandered back into the dark cool of his office and felt beneath the iron bunk inside a cell where he had been slumbering for — 'Jeez,' he said, 'can that be the time?' — two, no, three hours.

He hooked out the bottle of whiskey. There was two inches of the fiery brew left. He had a splitting headache and he felt like he must have swallowed one of the musty felt blankets in his sleep. 'Uk!' he gasped, as he glugged down a good bite, studied the remains, then finished it off. 'This stuff will be the death of me.'

Maybe it would, too, he thought, as he jerked a curly-brimmed Capper & Capper flat-crowned felt hat down over his forehead and looked at his sticky, shaking palm. He was in no condition for a gunfight so maybe it was just as well he had been asleep.

These thoughts in mind, he hitched on his gunbelt and scuffed his boots through the dust towards Tonio's saloon.

'Okay,' he boomed, shoving through the doorway, his eyes adjusting to the gloom. 'What's going on this time? You boys been havin' some fun?'

'You may well ask.' Harry Hall, the big, surly ramrodder out at the

Waterson spread, the biggest ranch on the Okinotchie River, got up from his knees. He had been trying to stanch the flow of blood from the wrist and calf of his boss's youngest son. 'That Mex, Estevan, came stormin' in and shot down the Kid here.'

'Yeah,' the Kid whined, still propped against the bar. 'He didn't give me a chance to draw. You better go bring him in, Sheriff.'

'Me an' whose army? You think I'm crazy? Anyway, you ain't dead, are yuh?' Steve gave a poke with his boot at the youth's thigh, making him yell piteously. 'No I didn't think so. More's the pity.'

'What did you say?' Harry growled, threateningly.

'You heard. If you were honest you would probably agree with me. Ain't you sick of wet-nursing this whiny little louse?'

The Kid's eyes swivelled upwards fearfully. 'I wouldn't let my father hear you say that, McCormack, or you'll be out of a job.'

'So what? You think that would be any hardship?' The sheriff stroked his unshaven jaw and put his rifle aside, propping it against the bar. 'OK, Tonio, set me a stiffener up. Ain't you got anything better than that potato lightning?'

'You wan' tequila?' The bar-owner smiled. 'Or maybe mescal?'

'No, whiskey'll do. Let's take the skin off my tonsils, old pal, once and for all. OK, Harry, let's hear your version of events. What's this all about?'

'Aw, Estevan reckons the Kid owes him a thousand dollars from some all-night poker-game. That's crazy. It's a fortune. No man's got that amount of loot. The Kid here was drunk as a 'coon, didn't know what was happening, just kept giving the Mexican promissory notes. He thought it was a big joke.'

'So, why ain't he laughing now?'

'Quit the jokes, Sheriff.' The Kid groaned as he was helped up. He hopped over to a chair. 'Somebody go get me the doc. I'm bleeding to death.'

'Might do you good to let a bit of alcohol outa your veins.' The sheriff took a more careful taste of the whiskey and shuddered. 'Christ, this stuff! Tonio, you oughta be forced to pay for the coffins of the men you've poisoned in here.'

'Listen who's talking.' Harry Hall beamed at the others. 'The pot calling the kettle black.'

'Yeah,' one of the ranch hands agreed. 'The state he's in, I bet he couldn't hit a barn door with that side-iron of his. No wonder he don't want to go after Estevan.'

Steve McCormack winced, but tried to ignore their jibes. Well, wasn't it the truth? The truth hurt, but a man had to face it. The whiskey had gotten a hold on him.

'Just one more,' he muttered to Tonio, pushing across his empty tumbler.

'Sure,' Harry sneered. 'And one more after that. And one more . . . some frigging sheriff you are. You can't back out of it, McCormack. You'd better get on your horse, if you can stay on, and ride down to the Ramirez spread and warn them to forget this foolishness.'

'I'm not so sure they will be persuaded.' Steve studied the fresh whiskey in his glass and gulped some back, waiting for it to explode in his insides. 'You see, where I come from a man honours his card debts, a gentleman, that is. Or anybody with any sense don't run 'em up in the first place. And in my opinion Estevan Ramirez will have the same strict views.'

'Hell, Sheriff, whose side you on?' the Kid called, angrily. 'Where can I get that kinda cash from? Like Harry says, it's just a joke. The most the old man would give me is a couple hundred. Look what that crazy greaser's done to me. And this ain't all. He's threatened to kill me. You got to stop him.'

Steve turned to face him, his lips pursed, considering the Kid. 'Look, you worm, I ain't paid to fight your battles. Anyway, if I know Estevan he ain't the

11

sort to shoot first without giving a man a chance to go for his gun.'

'You callin' me a liar, Sheriff?'

'Yep.' Steve took off his hat and tossed it on to the bar counter. 'I guess I am. You other men saw what happened. Who fired first here?'

Most shrugged, turned away, leaned on the bar. They had no wish to cross Old Man Waterson, the biggest cattle baron in those parts. Nor had they much sympathy for his youngest son.

'Well, your silence speaks for itself, don't it?'

'Maybe it does. Maybe it don't. That would have to be decided by the judge.' Hall picked up his rifle, and, his tattered leather chaps flapping, strode over and put out a hand to the Kid. 'Come on, you ain't dying. Them's only flesh wounds. The quack can tend you back at the ranch.'

He and another cowboy picked the Kid up and helped him hop to the swing-doors. They were followed by the dozen other ranch hands from the

12

Waterson spread. 'Get him on his horse.'

The ramrodder turned and scowled at McCormack. 'Estevan Ramirez carried out an unprovoked attack here. He's not only threatened to kill him, but to rustle our herd. It's up to you to put the lid on this, Steve. Or are you looking for range war?'

'Maybe,' one of his men jeered, 'he's just a Mex-lover.'

'Or sceered of 'em, more like,' another called.

Steve watched them go, then turned back to his drink.

'Hell take 'em,' he muttered as he tossed it back.

★    ★    ★

Silver City, where Steve McCormack was elected to keep the peace, had, as its name implied, once been a silver boomtown. But the lodes had run out and most of the mines were abandoned or flooded. A few prospectors still

13

hopefully worked on but hardly made enough to keep body and soul together. Most of the time the town was deathly peaceful and all Steve had to do was collect local taxes or keep an eye on any drifters who rode in. Usually, a warning to keep on moving would suffice for they weren't to know that often the young sheriff had difficulty getting his aim focused. He could hold his liquor without revealing his inebriation or flying thoughts, or so he hoped. Things hotted up, it had to be admitted, when cowpunchers from outlying ranches rode in to paint the town red and spend with abandon their monthly twenty dollars. At such times Steve would get himself a bottle and retire to his bunk until they'd drunk, gambled or whored away their last dime. Sometimes he was forced to lock up one or two of the more obstreperous in his hoosegow, but, fortunately, such cowboy high spirits rarely resulted in bloodshed. Of course, the sober citizens complained bitterly about harassment and being kept awake at night by the hullabaloo, but Steve managed to soothe the troubled waters and hang on to his badge. He had no real wish to vacate his job. The money wasn't so bad and it beat poking cows backsides out on the range. He was well aware that Old Man Waterson, as he was known, had only to lean on the town council members, the bunch of storekeepers who ran Silver City's affairs, if his anger was aroused, and he, Steve, would be given the bum's rush. That was why he regarded the antics of his youngest son, the Kid, as a real pain in the butt.

McCormack sat and pondered these facts over another bottle of red-eye that night, but he took it steady, lounged in a corner of Tonio's saloon, his Winchester propped by his side. He would drink himself out of this two-day spat. Why he had become a slave to whiskey he wasn't sure, and his thoughts drifted haphazardly, recalling his past wanderings. He had worked as drover, bank

15

guard, stage driver, cowpuncher, rail-road labourer, and at innumerable dead-end jobs to raise a few dollars when he was down and out before getting on his horse and rolling on. He could never, until now, stay one place long. He needed to see what was on the other side of the next hill. What had brought him to Silver City he had no idea, nor why he had stayed. He just had a hankering to put down roots, to make something of his life. But why here, nowhere, out in the wilds of New Mexico?

'Beats me,' he said, when he staggered back to his jailhouse to sleep off the booze. 'I gotta pull myself together in the morning. Go out, see what's going on.' Steve knew he could shoot well enough when he was sober. It was just a matter of staying off the bottle until this problem was resolved. 'I guess I'm too easy-going and peaceable-minded to be a lawman.' He was speaking to Jock, who was settling down with a scratch, sigh and grunt beside the bunk. 'I gotta start taking things more serious. We ain't gonna stand no nonsense from the Ramirezes, nor the Watersons, neither.'

In the morning he washed himself under the cold pump out in the yard, rinsed the cobwebs from his mind, shaved the week's growth of gleaming gold stubble from his jaw, tossed away his sweat-stained shirt and dressed in a clean woollen one, lilac in colour. He tucked it into his new-washed jeans, pulled on fringed shotgun-chaps, boots and spurs, and his brown leather topcoat, fastened his gunbelt, packed a few necessities, including a spare box of ammo, grabbed his hat, blanket-roll, and rifle, and went to saddle his mule, old Moose. The big, stiff-legged beast wasn't exactly beautiful, but he was dependable, and Steve would back him any day against a horse for long-distance stamina. He climbed aboard, swung him around, whistled to Jock, and set off at a lope out of town, across the plain in the direction he had seen Estevan disappear. The thirty-mile journey would take him most part of the day. It was rough country.

# 2

Old Man James Waterson had a face as hard and tanned as tooled saddle-leather, his receding silver hair falling back in quiffs around his pointed ears. His eyes were upward-turned, grey glints, accentuating a look people had often likened to a dark-skinned devil. And, like Satan himself, the wealthy rancher was uncompromising in his views. When he had returned from the Civil War, fighting in the eastern Mississippi campaign, he had carved out this land of his against the ravages of Apaches. He was wearing range clothes, pulling on his riding-gloves, as he stepped out from his wooden ranch house on to the veranda ready to give his men their morning orders.

'That's right, you take it easy.' He glanced along at his youngest son, Caleb, who was reclined on a bamboo chair with a footrest, nursing his bandaged calf. 'Don't you worry about doing any work to maintain this ranch. How long you think you goin' to be lying there on your backside for?'

'Don't start, Pa.' Caleb, or the Kid, as he was better known to all and sundry, was a softer version of his father, with the same, impish, upturned corners to his mouth and eyes. 'How can I work when I'm gunshot?'

'Whose damn fault is that? You brought misfortune upon yourself. I'm sick and tired of your damned scrapes. It's time you grew up, boy.'

'Hell, what you expect me to do, Pa? Estevan Ramirez was out to kill me. I had to defend myself.'

'You stir up that Ramirez hornet's nest we're in trouble. Ain't I always told you to steer clear of them. I've maintained an uneasy peace for years now and a nitwit like you has to spoil it all.'

'What you scared of, Pa? You're the big ex-soldier, aincha? A few greaser

20

scum shouldn't bother you.'

The Kid smirked, scratching at his bullet-shaped, close-cropped head, arranging his gangling limbs more comfortable as he reached for his mug of coffee. But the smirk disappeared as James Waterson strode across, grabbed at his fancy silk neckerchief, hauled his son out of the chair and sent him flying.

'Don't you ever speak to me again like that, you useless, cheeky pup.' Waterson's face was blood-red with anger under his tan. 'You ain't too old for a thrashing.'

'Christ!' The Kid let out a wail of pain, clutching his bandage as he sprawled on the veranda decking. 'You old bastard. Oh, my leg! Damn you! You ever touch me again I'm out of here.'

'Go and be damned, you drunken, idle piece of crowbait. You know where you'll end up, in the gutter or riding with some worthless outlaw gang, hunted from pillar to post. We won't

21

miss you. Jed here's worth a dozen of you.'

The Kid's older brother, Jed, was standing behind his father and could not help but smile, basking in his father's praise.

'I think you're right, Pa. Let him go. Let him see how he makes out on his own.'

'He's going nowhere.' The rancher's wife, Kathleen Waterson, had appeared from the house and her firm voice rang out. She was a middle-aged, pasty-faced woman, about 250 pounds in weight. She had a black shawl wrapped around a plain grey dress, and her greying hair was drawn back in a bun. 'Help your brother up, Jed. Can't you see he's an invalid?'

'I've had enough, Kathleen. He's no Waterson. He's just a wastrel. He can clear off and make his own bed. He'll soon come crawling back.'

'He's going nowhere,' she repeated, firmly. 'He's only a boy, James. Aren't you thankful he only has an injured leg?

What do you want, our son brought home dead on a stretcher?'

'That's what I'm trying to prevent, Kathleen. The way he's going that's what it will be.'

'You've always been so hard on him. Maybe that's why he's turned out like he has. He's got to rest that leg for a couple of weeks or more, Doc Stevens said so. There's no question about it. What are you *doing*, attacking him like that?'

The Kid had climbed on to the recliner with his brother's help, and it was his turn to smirk again.

'Yeah, Pa, can I help it I wasn't in the army? We can't all be war heroes. If *you* were? Sometimes I doubt it. Whose word we got for it? I'm sick of listening to you, old man.'

When Waterson gave a roar of rage and made a move towards him again, the Kid flinched, but his mother caught hold of her husband by the arm, restraining him.

'So help me,' Waterson fumed, 'one

of these days I'll — '

'Sure, attack me when I'm down,' his son sneered. 'I tell you what, I ain't scared of you, and I ain't scared of them greasers, neither. Sometimes I figure it's you who's the chicken.' The Kid whipped out his expensive Smith & Wesson, aimed at a bucket stood in the dust of the yard and sent it flying and spinning. *Blam! Blam! Blam!* The shots rang out. He grinned and spun the revolver on his finger. 'I coulda taken Estevan. He got the drop on me. And' — he waved the gun in his father's direction — 'I can take you, old man. You ever touch me again you'll find out.'

His father stood, shaking his head, puzzled.

'You ever point a gun at a man you better be prepared to use it,' he muttered.

'Come on, Pa,' Jed said, touching his father's arm. 'Leave him. You know he only riles you up. We got work to do.'

'Yes. Kathleen, you just carry on

soft-soaping that young layabout . . . well, don't say I haven't warned you.'

The Old Man, as most called him — or O.M. for short — turned on his heel, strode over to his horse and swung into the saddle.

'We'll be back at sundown.'

He rode out of the yard, stiff-backed, his soberly attired son, Jed, by his side, his men loping on their ponies after them.

'Yeah,' the Kid drawled. 'Good riddance. Don't hurry back, boys.'

'Why do you always have to ruck your father?' The burly mother went to her younger son's side, pouring him more coffee to refill the spilled mug, fussing around him. 'You know his temper.'

'Aw, he thinks he's so high and mighty. One of these days . . . '

'Now, you know you don't mean that. The O.M.'s only thinking of your own good. He's worried about you. Why do you always have to be at each other's throats?'

'The O.M.'s a pain, Ma. I'm grown

now. I'm telling you he better never not touch me again. I won't be accountable. So help me, Ma, I'll kill him.'

'Rubbish. Your father needs you and you need him. We've all got to stick together.'

'Yeah, sure.'

★ ★ ★

The sky was a saucer of blue, empty but for a Swainson's hawk that hovered searching for prey, and the temperature was in the nineties Fahrenheit. This heat sure sweats the whiskey out of a man, Steve thought, as he followed a tortuous trail, deeply rutted over the years by wagon-wheels, which wound through the barren canyons and *barrancas* of this part of New Mexico.

'Black, black is the colour of my true love's hair'. The sheriff began singing to raise his spirits 'Her lips are sweet and rosy fair; The purtiest face and daintiest hands, I love the prairie on where she stands.'

His song came to an abrupt end as he heard voices up ahead of him, and, with natural caution, he loosened his Winchester in the saddle boot. When he topped a rise he saw the cause of the raised voices: a stagecoach, drawn by four horses, was keeled over at an angle and two men were examining a rear wheel which had gone adrift.

Strange that he had been singing that popular refrain because standing beside them was a slim young woman in a purple dress and travelling-cape, her shimmering crown of black hair cascading half-way down her back.

As he rode nearer on his mule he realized that she was a Latino girl, but far more beautiful than any of that race he had seen around these parts. For a start she was petite and slender, whereas many hereabouts inclined to stoutness. But, if slim, she had plenty of flesh filling out her costume in the right places. Her heart-shaped face was, indeed, the prettiest he had seen in many a day, her hands the daintiest, and a man might even say her expressive lips were 'something rosy fair'.

'Howdy,' he called, recognizing the driver and guard of the stage line. 'You got trouble, I see.'

He tipped a finger to his hat to the young woman. '*Buenos dias, señorita.*'

Her dark eyes were wide-set and her brow middling high, as if she'd got plenty of thinking-room behind there. Suddenly the cynical and world-weary sheriff found a new spark of interest in life. She was some humdinger, that was for sure, but a tad cool and arrogant with it, too, as if she knew her worth.

'*Buenos dias,*' she murmured.

'Howdy Sheriff,' the driver gruffly replied. 'The axle's snapped clean in half. Hell take this lousy trail.'

'What brings you out here? This is off your usual beat, ain't it?'

'We're taking this young lady to the Ramirez ranch. Or, we was.'

'The Ramirez ranch. That's where I'm heading. You a friend of the family?'

'No, I am family. I am the daughter of Señor Ramirez.'

'You are? Well, I heard he had a gal, but I never thought — '

'Thought what?' she challenged.

'Thought . . . ' he changed tack, 'to meet you like this.'

'Did I hear them say you are a sheriff? If so, what business have you with my father?'

'It ain't with your father. It's with your brother, Estevan. He shot a man yesterday. I gotta kinda read him the riot act.'

'Shot? You mean killed him?'

'No, shot him in the leg. He's OK, but there's more to it than that.'

'It don't look like we're goin' to be able to fix this. We're gonna have to go back to Silver City, get the blacksmith to come out.' The driver tipped his battered hat over his forehead and scratched the back of his head. 'Maybe it's lucky you come along, Sheriff. Maybe you could give the lady a ride to her destination.'

'I'd be glad to give the young lady a ride any time she wants one.' Steve's pale-blue eyes sparkled lecherously. 'If she ain't got any objection to gittin' up on my moth-eaten mule?'

Señorita Ramirez glanced at the slim sheriff, at his panting wolfhound and his solid mule, hesitantly.

'A ride's a ride,' she said, with a sudden frankness in her smile.

'I guess I could let you ride while I walk, but we got ten more miles to go, and I ain't never been keen on shanks's pony.' He held out a gloved hand. 'You comin' up?'

The girl reached up and their grips locked.

'Right? Hup!' he called, and swung her to sit sidesaddle behind him. 'You better hang on to my waist, *señorita*. It's a bumpy trail, and a mule ain't as comfortable a ride as a hoss.'

Tentatively, she placed her hands on his hips and called, 'Don' worry, I'm used to riding donkeys.'

'It ain't a donkey. It's a mule.'

'I know, but I'm saying I had a donkey when I was a girl.'

'Right, just hang on tight as you like. I take it you boys'll ride the coach horses back to Silver City. *Adios, amigos.*'

He set off on up the trail through the rugged mountain pass and the girl gave a little yelp of concern as the mule lurched. She did as he suggested: grabbed hold of him tighter.

'That's fine, Miss Ramirez, just hang on tight as you like. It's kinda nice.'

As they bumped along on the rough trail the girl could not help her body, or bosom even if constrained by her dress, and hard as she tried to hold back — from pressing against the man's broad back. To feel the bouncy warmth of her against him, the touch of her hands, had the sudden effect of sending a shudder, like electricity, through him. 'Hell,' he muttered, trying to keep his mind on the road. 'This sure is cosy, *señorita.*'

'No need to be so formal, sheriff,' she

31

called out. 'My name is Madalena.'

'Pleased to meetcha, Madalena. Call me Steve.'

Why am I gettin' in a lather about this gal? the thought suddenly occurred to him. I ain't got no chance. She's a Ramirez. You think they're gonna let her get acquainted with a drunken saddlebum sheriff and a gringo to boot?

'Hell, I better watch what I do.'

'What's that you say?' she called out as the mountain wind whipped his muttered words away.

'Aw, forget it,' he said, trying to relax.

'My father can send a buggy out to collect my trunk.'

'Yeah, I guess.' What, he wondered, was he going to say to her father, *Don* Luis Ramirez, who reigned like a feudal lord in this mountain terrain? What say to Estevan, except try to make him cool his hot head?

'Estevan has always been wild,' the girl shouted to him. 'But he is not bad. You won't arrest him will you, Steve?'

'I fancy not,' he called back as they

went at a stiff trot through the pass. 'I don't think that's exactly feasible right now. Come on, Jock,' he shouted. 'Leave that jack-rabbit alone.'

'I've never heard of a sheriff who took his dog along on a job before.'

'Waal,' he drawled, 'you have now. How come you're such a classy-looking gal? You been visiting the city?'

'Yes, I've been away three years at college.'

'You glad to be home again?'

'So-so,' she shrugged. 'In some ways yes, in some ways no. Is it a home or a prison?'

'Oh, I see. Well it looks like a damn fortress to me,' he said, as the Rancho Ramirez building, its adobe walls glowing ruddy in the setting sun, came into view.

The main ranch house was a low-slung building, its eight-feet thick adobe walls glowing blood-red in the rays of the westering sun. Castellated defence works surrounded its flat roof, a reminder of the days not long before when the full moon brought terror as the Apache raided. These days Geronimo and his braves kicked their heels in Florida dungeons. Most others of their tribe were confined on reservations, the braves forced to wear hated distinguishing tags around their necks. Some renegades still lurked in the higher reaches of the mountains, but it was safe enough to assume the Apache had been beaten into submission after 300 years of bitter fighting.

Steve had crossed the Burro mountains south-west of Silver City and entered an area of tangled mountain and desert clothed only by cactus and sagebrush where humankind were few and far between. But now the yucca, stones and mesquite gave way to a valley, a tributary of the Upper Gila river, where grama grass grew up to the bellies of the longhorn cattle which grazed and watered along the river edge.

'It may be wild,' the girl suddenly cried, 'but it's home.'

'Yeah,' Steve grunted, 'and there ain't no place like home.'

Beyond the ranch rose mountain ranges through which passes wound into the territory of Arizona, and to the south could be seen the stark peaks of remote and forbidding ranges which marked that other frontier of Old Mexico.

The whole south-west corner of New Mexico had long been the haunt of outlaws and smugglers, petty criminals and rustlers who, if sighted, were given short shrift by the Ramirezes guns, as they were to find out. Steve nudged his mule through clumps of glowering cattle and forded the Ramirez river, but as they went splashing up on to the far bank a rifle shot cracked out and lead chiselled a boulder close by the mule's fore hoofs, making sparks fly. The sheriff reined in hard and Moose gave vent to his irritation by loud and prolonged brays.

A low growl curled in Jock's throat and the hairs on his scruff bristled as four riders appeared galloping towards them down from a rocky ridge. Attired in sombreros and the garb of *vaqueros* they all brandished arms and looked like they meant business.

'OK, boy,' Steve snapped at the wolfhound. 'Hold it. And you' — he slapped at the mule's jaw — 'for Chrissakes quit your braying.'

The leading rider drew in before them in a swirling of dust, a snarl of distaste on his face as he examined the gringo, which broke into a smile as Madalena laughed and called out, 'Hi, Emilio.'

'What are you doing here — with him?'

'I wanted to surprise you,' she replied in Spanish, 'but the stage broke down. This gentleman came to my rescue.'

'But, sister, you are supposed to be . . .'

'Yes, I know but I finished early.'

The other three *vaqueros* were staring at her with some astonishment, lowering their rifles.

'You had better get down from there,' Emilio said, 'before Father sees you.'

'Nonsense. Are you still so suspicious of Americanos? Haven't you learned that we have to live with them?'

'We trust no gringo. You should not ride with such an *hombre*.'

'Don't be silly. Out of the way, Emilio,' she cried. 'I have had a long journey. This is Steve. He is sheriff at Silver City.'

'*Sí*, I know him. What does he want here?'

'He has business with Estevan.'

'Ha! You hear that, boys? The sheriff thinks he can come riding in here with my sister behind him and arrest my brother.'

The *vaqueros* laughed, but spun their horses around and went forward at a lope, shouting out the news as they approached the outer wall of the ranch house and rode through the gate. Women washing clothes at a rock 'tank' looked up with smiles of surprise and waved to Madalena as others ran to greet her, men, women and children.

Steve rode his mule up to the studded door of solid oak at the front of the ranch house, which opened, and an older man, in ornately embroidered, tight-fitting Mexican costume, stepped outside, his thick silver hair flowing back from a face as harsh-cut as dark mahogany. The sheriff recognized Señor Luis Enrique Ramirez, who gave him a withering glance, before raising a hand to his daughter.

'Madalena!'

'Father.' She slipped down from the mule and hugged herself into him. 'I'm home.'

'Let me look at you.' He held her at arm's length. 'Three years. I hardly recognized you. You depart a girl and return a young woman.'

'Yeah,' Steve drawled, 'and quite a sassy one.'

Ramirez drew his daughter into his side and scowled at him. 'Who asked your opinion gringo?? What do you want here?'

'I want a few words with you, Señor Ramirez, and with your son, Estevan.'

'You, who are you? You think that tin star gives you authority here? We don't need you. The only law here is made by our rifles.'

'Father, Steve helped me. I would have been stranded. Is this any way to greet him?'

'Why did you not tell me you were coming home? I would have sent an armed escort to Silver City to greet you. Instead you arrive out of the blue riding behind this' — his face gave a grimace of distaste — 'this so-called sheriff.'

'Hey, I come here for a friendly talk, thassall,' Steve gritted out. 'But I oughta point out that you're a citizen of the United States these days, señor, and, as such, you and your boys have to abide by the laws of the USA.'

'New Mexico is not a state,' Emilio put in. 'It is only a territory.'

'It amounts to the same thing. If you people think you can still live by the gun and are immune to the law, you're mistaken.'

'Go to hell,' the older Ramirez snapped. 'You will never touch or speak to my daughter again. You will do so at your peril.'

'Father!' Madalena protested, tugging at his arm. 'Is this how you greet me? The sheriff rescued me. He has had a long ride. You can, at least, talk to him, show him some hospitality.'

'We have no wish to give hospitality to gringos. But' — Ramirez hugged her to him — 'this is a joyous occasion. Have him brought in. I will hear what he has to say.'

# 3

Guitars, reed pipes and an Indian drum pounded out a fast fandango as Señor Ramirez and his *vaqueros* feasted under the starry sky on the terrace of his adobe mansion. As this was a special occasion the men and women, young and old, who worked in the house and in the fields, had been invited to join in the festivities. They sat along trestle-tables under oil-flares, laughing and singing out as they demolished wild turkey in a thick hot sauce, egg-plant fried with red peppers, *tortillas* laced with onions and garlic, chopped pork with salads of tomatoes and olives, bread fresh-baked in a big stone oven, and goat-cheese. The *haciendado* had provided a huge cask from his cellar from which rough red wine flowed copiously.

Steve took a good swallow of the

musky liquid and sighed with satisfaction. After a long ride in the hot sun this was indeed a fine ending to the day. If it was the end? He glanced, a tad uneasily, at Luis Enrique's two sons, Emilio and Ramon, sprawled amid their *vaqueros* and already looking more than a little excited by the alcohol. He raised his red-and-black clay tumbler to the rancher, and to his daughter, who sat beside him.

'*Salud*! You folks sure know how to do yourselves well.'

Madalena smiled widely. 'I can assure you we don't eat and drink like this every day.'

Many of the peons, men and women, were by now involved in a whirling, raucous dance, snapping their fingers, stomping their bootheels and giving wild, shrieking birdlike calls. Steve got to his feet and grinned at her.

'Howja like to step it out, *señorita*?'

Her father's countenance froze with anger as he raised his hand. 'Haven't I told you, mister, you are here under sufferance. You will not — '

'Oh, come on, Papa. It is my homecoming. The sheriff means no harm. Surely, one little dance?' Before Ramirez could protest further she had slipped away across the terrace, beckoning Steve with her eyes, to stand poised at the edge of the mob of dancing bodies.

Steve touched a finger to his hat brim to the *haciendado*, who tossed his white hair haughtily, anger seething in him. The young sheriff ambled over to Madalena, took her fingers in one hand and placed his other hand around her waist.

'I ain't so hot at this Spanish stuff but maybe I can teach ya the Texas two-step?'

With which he whirled her into the throng, kicking up his bootheels and joining in the yells. 'Yip! Yai! Yai! Yee!'

Madalena, dressed now in a modest traditional *huipil*, a white blouse with bright-red thread embroidery, and bell-shaped satin skirt, laughed as she hung on to him.

'If my classmates could see me now! We were taught to dance in a more civilized way.'

'How come a gal like you's learned all them fancy Yankee ways then comes back to live in the wilds?'

'It was my mother's wish. She wanted me to absorb some of her own people's culture. She was an American.'

'Ah, that accounts for it. Your looks. You ain't fully fledged Mexican. Where is she?'

'My mother? She died of a fever four years ago.'

'Ah, too bad.' He swung her around but in a more gentle manner, glancing at her face. 'What kinda fever?'

'The doctor said it was malaria caused by bad airs, miasmas from swamps. But it is very dry air here in the mountains.'

'Ah, yes, but the latest thinking seems to be that malaria might be caused by mosquito bites.'

Madalena tilted her head, holding herself apart and smiled inquisitively.

'So the sheriff knows a little more of the world than horses or guns?'

'I got plenty time to read the journals. Some professor reckons that death from 'skeeters' bites was the third biggest cause of death, apart from bullets and bombs, in the Big War. The first biggest killer was chronic dire-rear and typhoid second.'

'Really?'

'Yep.'

He grinned at her, gripped her tight, whirling her fast into the flowing fandango, making her squeal and her skirt cartwheel to reveal its crimson lining.

Suddenly a gunshot crashed out, bringing the commotion of dancers and drinkers to a halt. A young man in a wide sombrero had ridden into the dusty courtyard on a blue-eyed, grey stallion. He held one of his smoking Colt Lightning .38s pointed at the sky. The oil-flares slopped shadows over the faces of the startled dancers as Madalena hung on to Steve McCormack and cried out, 'Estevan!'

Her elder brother pointed his revolver at the American and sneered, 'What is he doing here? What are you doing dancing with a Yankee? Has everyone gone mad?'

'Hold it, Estevan,' his father rapped out. 'We will have no shooting, no bloodshed tonight. This is Madalena's homecoming party. It was her request that he be our guest. Without his help she would not have got here.'

'Have you, too, gone soft in the head, Father? You invite a Yankee to our festivities? You allow him to dance with my sister?'

'Come on, pal.' Steve stepped forward, his palms spread, appealing to him. 'Get off your high horse. You're spoiling the party. Anyhow, I ain't no Yankee. I'm from the South. And I ain't here to arrest you. I'm just here to issue a warning.'

'A warning?' The handsome Latino slipped his revolver back into its holster. '*You* come here to warn *me*?'

'You could call it a legally official caution. You . . . '

Estevan reached for a twelve-foot woven rawhide bullwhip coiled on his pommel. 'Here is *my* warning to *you*.' The whip snaked out, its leaden tip cutting a bloody gash from the sheriff's cheek. He cracked the whip like a revolver shot again as Madalena screamed. But this time Steve was ready for the flashing whip. He ducked and snatched at it. It burned his palms but he hung on and gave it a hard jerk, toppling Estevan from his saddle. He looped the thong around the Latino's throat as he tried to scramble up and pulled it tight. Estevan struggled, gasping, his face colouring up under his dark skin, but he was at a disadvantage. Steve could have throttled him if he had wished to.

'Don't ever try giving me a whupping again,' he gritted out, applying pressure. 'Or I'll damn well kill you.'

Estevan clawed his fingers at the noose tightening around his throat. The sheriff loosened the pressure and tossed the whip contemptuously away. 'You understand?'

'Sí,' Estevan croaked out. 'OK.' He climbed to his feet, his face livid, his pride badly hurt. As the young sheriff went to move away Estevan grabbed hold of his shirt with his left hand and smashed his right fist into Steve's jaw. 'It's you who will be killed.'

Caught off balance McCormack back-pedalled and crashed on to a trestle-table, scattering a bowl piled with fruit. He raised his boots as Estevan rushed him and kicked hard back. It was Estevan's turn to do a backward somersault. The sheriff's dander was up. He pounced on him and smacked him with every inch of his strength across the jaw. Estevan's head snapped back. But he managed to clamber to his feet and they began pounding blows at each other.

'Stop it!' Madalena was screaming, trying to intervene.

'Enough!' her father shouted.

Estevan was backing off, mainly because the huge wolfhound, seeing his master in trouble, had bounded into the affray, his throat booming a warning, his fangs bared, going for the Latino, who, his face tense, reached for his left-hand twin revolver to defend himself.

'Jock! Down!' Steve snapped, grabbing at his collar. 'Leave him, boy,' he said, as he hauled the hound off. 'Come on, I can fight my own battles.'

Madalena had to smile. 'I see now why you have him around.'

Estevan's companions caught hold of his arms, pulled him away, tried to soothe him, and, much flustered, he put away the Lightning, ran fingers through his hair, picked up his sombrero, and scowled at the American, trying to salvage his pride.

'Well,' Steve drawled, touching the blood on his cheek, tenderly, 'I guess we're *both* warned, ain't we? And both scarred.'

The *haciendado* had risen from his

seat and taken Estevan into a corner, lecturing him. 'You have abused my laws of hospitality. This man is not to be attacked while he is with us. Now I am going to speak with him, try to straighten out this matter.'

Luis Enrique Ramirez, in his embroidered velveteens, stroked back his white mane and beckoned to the sheriff.

'You, come with me. The rest of you, carry on with the feast.'

He led Steve into the house and sat him down in a chair made of horn and hide beside a long banqueting table. He stood in front of a wide fireplace and folded his arms across his chest.

'My son is very hot-blooded.'

'You coulda fooled me,' Steve muttered, dabbing at the blood on his cheek.

'Sometimes I have difficulty restraining him. He is incensed about the money the Waterson boy owes him.'

'The Kid? You know yourself he's full of piss an' prune-juice. He was liquored up that night. He didn't know what he was doing, thought it some sorta joke. Can't Estevan see that?'

'No. He says he wants the money. Or else he . . . '

'Yeah, I've heard his threats. Is that what you want, *señor*? War?'

'Naturally not. I realize the old days are gone. We cannot settle all our disputes with guns. That is foolishness. Too many men will die on both sides. But, I fear I cannot control him and his brothers. I need your help, Sheriff.'

'That's what I'm here for, to talk some horse sense.'

'No, you are the paid lackey of Waterson. You are on his side. *He* has sent you to warn us. Maybe he *wants* to get us mad?'

'Don't be a fool. I'm on nobody's side. I'm on the side of law and order, thassall. I don't want no bloodshed, same as you. I've got a nice li'l peaceful town to look after.'

'You cannot deny you are his lackey. He pays the town council who pay your wages.' The old man eyed him severely, and went to a cabinet. He took out a tin box and removed the lid. 'Here,' he pressed a leather pouch into the sheriff's palm. He closed Steve's fingers over it. 'One hundred dollars in gold pieces. You will get the same next month. And the month after that. Now you work for me. You will do as *I* tell you, not Waterson.'

'Hey, hold on. I don't want this.' Steve tossed the pouch on to the table. 'Maybe Waterson does, in some ways, keep me in my job, but I ain't for sale to the highest bidder.'

'Is not enough? You want two hundred?'

'Look, if you got all this cash to toss around why don't you let me arrange for a thousand from you to be given to the Kid on condition he repays it to Estevan and makes some kinda apology? That way you'll get your cash back. You won't lose a son to a bullet. Nobody's a loser.'

Señor Ramirez considered this proposal. 'No. I do not trust the Kid. He would take the money and laugh at us. I would be throwing away a thousand dollars.'

'Not if I arranged the meeting, didn't give him the cash until just before the meet. It would look as if he was finally doing the honourable thing and everybody's pride would be satisfied.'

'No. I will give you the thousand dollars. I and my sons will go south of the border. We need to buy horses. While we are away you will kill the Kid. The thousand in gold will be yours. You can head on out of this territory'

'Are you jokin'? I'm a sheriff not an assassin.'

'Hey, *hombre*, you're nothing, just a drunk and a drifter. And the Kid is a pile of horseshit. A trouble-maker. You know that yourself. You would be doing the world a favour if you shot him down.'

'No way, mister. In fact, I oughta report this conversation to the proper authorities. I'm sorry, *señor*, but you're gonna have to buy another shootist. I guess I gotta warn you that if the Kid should be gunned down under mysterious circumstances it's you I'm gonna come looking for.'

'How dare you? You're nothing . . . nobody. Get out of here! Now! Remember, if you think you can take me on, you think wrong. I will break you.'

'Waal,' Steve drawled, scratching his jaw, 'I'm sorry, and the reason I said I'm sorry is because I admire your daughter. She seems to be one Ramirez with an ounce of sense in her head. She's a fine girl. Think of her *señor*. Do you want her involved in this feud?'

'Get out! Take your mule and your hound and go. I guarantee you safe passage out of my lands. But, I warn you, you try to contact my daughter ever again, try to speak to her, or see her, you will die, bloodily. She is not for the likes of you.'

Steve pursed his lips and frowned. 'Listen, *señor*, if I want to see her again I *will* do. Your threats ain't gonna stop me.'

# 4

'Well, it's a fine how d'ye do,' Steve McCormack muttered to Jock as he hobbled the mule and scuffed around in a declivity in the rock to make a nest for the night. 'Here's me found the first gal I ever really fancied and she's on the other side of the fence. It ain't gonna be easy gittin' to her.'

Old Moose was braying his indignation at having his front hoofs roped together, so, if he wanted to get around, he had to hop in a most undignified manner.

'Shut up,' Steve shouted. 'You think I want to go searching for you in the marnin'? Sure, you'd like to be back in your stable but so would we all. A fool's a fool, unlikely to change, and a mule's a mule for ever.'

What sort of fool, he wondered, was he, to wander into this mess? A blood-feud about to blow up and him in the middle of it. Maybe he should have taken Don Luis Ramirez's gold and moseyed on. A thousand dollars was more loot than most men saved in a lifetime. It would buy him a nice little spread someplace. It was easy enough to kill a man. You just aimed your piece and pulled the trigger. Hadn't he shot down a ruffian who tried to hold up the stage when he was the shotgun guard? Hadn't he killed three Mexicans who tried to rustle the herd of a rancher he worked for? Hadn't he battled it out, lead for lead, with the desperado Sombrero Jack when he robbed the Silver City bank? He had had no qualms about that.

So what was Kid Waterson, as the *haciendado* said, but a nasty, boastful, bullying bit of walking offal that the world could well do without?

Why had he reached so vigorously to the *mordida*? The bribe? Was he a man who could afford such high principles? He had to admit that he had been surprised that Ramirez had offered it. He seemed a man of more upright demeanour. Maybe he was just trying to save them all a lot of trouble?

There was only a sliver of moon in the sky, often veiled by clouds, and it was too dark to risk riding for fear the mule might break a leg in this rough country of sharp boulders and potholes. They had reached a vast empty tract of high desert that looked more as though they were living on another planet than in the known world. At this altitude the soil was chill to lie upon. By noon it would be so hot it would burn the skin.

Steve wrapped himself in his own blanket and put the saddle blanket underneath for warmth, lay back on the saddle and turned up the collar of his leather coat.

'Let's git some shut-eye, eh, boy?'

The big, gangling dog curled up beside him and gazed dolefully his way.

'Don't blame me. At least they give us a good supper, didn't they?'

He had been getting soft, sleeping the

sleep of the oblivious drunkard in his jailhouse. It was time he got used to roughing it again. What was there to worry about? Only the night-time predators who had lain low under their stones during the heat of the day? Eight-inch centipedes with their toxic mandibles? Black widow spiders whose bite would give lethal stomach cramps? Mountain lions on the prowl? Huge, hairy tarantulas nosing about? Kissing bugs that could draw blood, cause irritation and nerve damage? Rattlers with heat-seeking mechanisms, which could strike in darkness? Or even the jolly old Gila monster, a two-feet lizard with bone-crushing jaws, its bite reputed to be deadly poisonous?

'No, nothing to worry about,' he muttered, pulling his hat down over his eyes. Except, maybe, human predators, the badhats and *viciosos* who drifted through these passes out of Mexico, and would gladly slit a man's throat as he slept.

But it wasn't these thoughts that kept

58

him from sleep. Nor the animation still coursing through him from his fight with Estevan Ramirez. No, it was the memory of *her*, Madalena, that kept him awake, exciting him, making his mind whirl with fantasies, thoughts of seeing her again, being together, making love, ideas that could never materialize. 'It's no good,' he groaned. 'I gotta forget her.

All in all he didn't have a very restful night and was glad of the glimmer of dawn. He found some dried tinder among the sagebrush and got a small fire going to boil water in his enamel coffee-pot. He squatted by the fire and warmed himself, sipping from his tin mug, and chewed on a strip of beef jerky, tossing a chunk to Jock and giving the mule a handful of split corn.

'Right, let's be heading back,' he said, tightening the latigo strap and swinging into the saddle.

The fire was a mistake. *Puh-tchoo*! That was the sound the bullet made as it came whining and spinning past his head to chisel rock. And another. *Padang!* — bouncing off his swinging coffee-pot. That was too close for comfort. The mule was bucking and hee-hawing his startled terror, and it was all Steve could do to hold him back, and drag him into the shade of a big rock.

'Shuddap, you idiot. Whoa, boy! Quit it! That ain't gonna help us.' He quietened the mule and tied his reins to an ocotillo bush as lead whined past them. 'Where the hell is he?'

He eased his Winchester out of the saddle boot, crept away to another position and peered from behind a smaller rock up at the puffs of black powder-smoke on the hillside. It looked like just one shootist. That was something to be thankful for. If there were more of them his chances would not be rosy. He rested the rifle's barrel on the rock and squinted along the sights, firing a fast succession of shots when he thought he saw movement among the bushes.

'Two can play at this game,' he muttered.

He took a cardboard box holding a dozen cartridges from the patch-pocket of his leather coat, and began to feed them into the magazine of the Winchester. They were .44–60 calibre and at close range would make a big hole in anybody. The octagonal-barrelled rifle was the latest on the market and probably the finest weapon ever produced by any company. He had only spent five but he wanted to keep the 14-shot stocked up. He debated whether to tie up the wolfhound or take him with him. He did not want him to get hurt, but, on the other hand, if he, himself, was killed he did not relish Jock being left tied to a tree at the mercy of mountain pumas.

'Come on, you dumb hick. We're gonna try to get up round the back of this lousy bushwhacker. See if you can keep your head down, if that's a possibility.'

He sprinted out from the rock diagonally left and upwards, the huge wolfhound bounding after him, passing him and leaping onward as if this was some sort of game. Their assailant began firing immediately, the shots cracking out, spurting dust by Steve's boots and whining away, ricocheting off the rocks.

The sheriff slid into the cover of a patch of mesquite amid boulders and ducked down, wincing, as bullets buzzed about his head like angry bees. Jock jumped back down beside him and licked at his ear.

'Waal, we got a second thing in our favour, pal, he ain't a great shot. You or me shoulda been dead by now.' He peered through the rocks and loosed two more bullets at the point where the black smoke drifted. He didn't expect to get lucky. He just wanted to draw the man's fire. He had counted twelve shots so far. There was no instant reply, so perhaps he had an older-style rifle. It was a chance he had to take because they would make an easy target over the next open stretch up the mountainside.

'Let's go,' he shouted and raced out, his boots slipping and sliding on the rocks and dust as he tried to make purchase and haul himself up the steep slope. Humming-birds scattered from the pink summer flowers as he ploughed into a clump of ocotillo. He was gasping for breath. It occurred to him he was out of condition.

'I gotta give up the whiskey,' he wheezed. 'It's killin' me.'

But, at least, his hunch had paid off. The would-be assassin must have been re-stocking his magazine for he suddenly started firing again, angrily and futilely.

'Stay!' He pointed a gloved finger at the hound. He had taught him to remain until he was called. Jock sat upon his haunches watching him as he crawled away up through the boulders and bushes. He wasn't wagging his tail; he seemed to sense the seriousness of this occasion.

Steve's coat, shotgun-chaps and gloves protected him from the worst of the cactus thorns, but it was hard work crawling upwards, the rifle in his hands. Finally he made it to a ridge and two bullets spat past his head as he rolled over into cover.

'Yah! Missed me,' he shouted, grinning to himself, and gave a whistle to the dog. He poked his hat upon his rifle barrel to cause a distraction and sure enough it went spinning as the dog came bounding up to join him. 'Ye're gittin' better,' he yelled up to whoever was hidden in the rocks now only about two hundred yards off. 'That was my best Capper & Capper ye've ruined.' He repeated the message in frontier Spanish, the words bouncing back and forth off the canyon walls. He wanted to try to pinpoint the man, but there was no response.

Steve picked up his Capper & Capper and examined the hole, then stuck it back on his head. About fifty yards above him was an overhang of dry sandstone cliff. If he could haul himself up there he would be able to reach the rocks piled by indiscriminate nature along the top of the hill and, hopefully, stalk whoever had a grudge against him. This was no ordinary highway robber.

It took all his strength and lean wiriness to work his way up the cliff-face, his fingers clinging to cracks in the rocks as he hoped against hope there were no snakes basking in the sun's rays that pounded into him. Twice the pointed toes of his high-heeled boots slipped and he had to hold himself upright by the power of his arms and fingers as sweat dripped into his eyes. But, somehow, he made it.

The wolfhound was bounding about below, whimpering, unable to climb the cliff. He cocked his head. Maybe this was a new game? But his master didn't have time to talk to him. He rolled over on to the cliff top, quickly unslinging the rifle from his back and levering in a slug. His assailant would, he imagined, be searching for him. This was going to be a cat-and-mouse game. He climbed up on to the jumbled pile of rocks, leaping from the peak of one to the other, peering about him and down below. He reached a flatter rock overlooking where the shots had been coming from and cautiously knelt down. As he did so a bullet whistled past him, cutting through the arm of his leather jacket as, simultaneously, he heard the crash of the explosion.

Steve spun around and saw the Mexican with a revolver in his grip, spurting fire. He gritted his teeth, squeezing out lead from the Winchester, levering in another slug, firing again from the hip with the natural ease of an experienced marksman. And he saw his second slug plough home. The man, little more than thirty feet away, opened his mouth in a rictus of pain, his revolver falling from his outstretched fingers, and, as if in slow motion, he spun around and topped over the cliff edge, shouting out in terror and agony as he fell away.

'Happy landing, pal,' the sheriff

drawled, as he jumped down to the cliff edge and watched the man's body go bouncing and tumbling down through the scree of rocks, half-way to the point where he had left his mule. 'It was you or me.'

He searched around at the top of the cliff until he found the Mex's hidey hole and his abandoned rifle with its scattering of used brass casings. Not one to waste a good rifle, he took it with him as he climbed down the mountainside by an easier route, leading the man's mustang.

Jock was standing on the fallen assailant's chest but he need not have bothered because he was unconscious.

'Leave him.' Steve studied the Mexican's dark, cadaverous face. 'Ramon?'

The bullet had crashed into his abdomen leaving a bloody hole. But it had not gone through him. It must have hit bone, possibly the hip, and been deflected. It was still lodged somewhere inside. The fall had not helped, either, adding cuts and bruises to his body, tearing his clothes.

Ramon groaned and flickered open his eyes, then clutched his torn abdomen as if he would like to hold in the blood flowing from it. He squealed like a stuck pig, whether from terror or pain, and lay, panting, staring pleadingly at the young sheriff.

'You got a belly-ache you ain't gonna recover from.' Steve pulled out his revolver, cocked the Colt Lightning with his thumb and put it to Ramon's temple. 'I've a mind to finish you. It would be kinder. You got any last words, like who sent you?'

'No, pliz, no!' the injured man hissed. 'Pliz don' keel me.'

'Waal, wouldn't that be natural justice? It's what you been tryin' to do to me. I said, who sent you?'

'Nobody send me. I do this, myself,' Ramon groaned. 'You shamed my brother, Estevan, in front of his people. You theenk you can have my seester. I avenge my family.'

'You ain't done much avenging so

far.' Steve slowly released the hammer. 'But you sure dumped me in the shit with your sister. She ain't gonna like me for killing her brother. What the hell shall I do with you? Leave you here for the buzzards?'

'No, pliz,' Ramon moaned. 'Pliz help me.'

'Shee-it! You're really asking some favour. Go back and face your gun-slinging brothers? You must be crazy.'

He stuffed the spare rifle under the cinch of the mustang — his hunch had been right, it was a 12-shot — and went to get his mule.

'Or is it me who's crazy as a loon at full moon?' he asked his hound as he rode back towards the hacienda.

He had patched Ramon up as best he could, stuffing his neckerchief into the wound to try to plug the escaping blood. He had given him water and hoisted him on to his mustang. Ramon had collapsed over its neck, barely able to hold on, so Steve had tied his bootheels with his lariat beneath the horse's belly and his wrists around his neck. 'I guess I must be,' he concluded.

His own throat had gone dry at the prospect of his reception as he rode determinedly back into the Ramirez territory. He looked up at the blue sky. It might well be the last day he saw it. The vision of his six-year-old son appeared in his mind, his tousled hair, his frank blue eyes, pleading, 'You will come home one day, won't you, Pa?' The boy lived with his mother and his new stepfather in El Paso. Tears welled up in Steve's own blue eyes as he thought of him, for he had seen armed *vaqueros* riding hard towards him. 'No, Jack, I guess maybe I might not be able to make it,' he whispered. 'Sorry.'

He truly believed they would shoot him down when they saw the burden carried by the mustang he was leading. Resolute, as if oblivious to their angry shouts as they gathered around, he rode on. They splashed back across the river and on towards the fortified adobe mansion, glowing roseate in the early-morning sun's rays. There were other harsh cries. People ran out on foot as he approached and viewed with awe the mangled remains of their master's dying son. He rode on through them and stepped down outside the big studded door as it was opened and Don Luis appeared, a shocked look on his face.

Steve McCormack shrugged his arms with exasperation and glanced at him.

'He tried to kill me. What could I do?'

Like an automaton, he ignored the bustle of people, cut Ramon free, caught him and laid him as gently as possible on the ground. The young man was still alive, groaning feebly, but Steve didn't hold out much hope. It was just a matter of time.

'I'm sorry,' he said, as he swung back on to his mule. 'I truly am.'

The mob of peons was getting vicious, calling for his blood, an eye for an eye.

'Kill the gringo,' several shouted.

'No.' Don Luis held up his hand. 'Leave him be.'

Estevan had galloped up on his horse. 'You are not going to let him go? We must be avenged, father.'

'No,' the old man shouted. 'I forbade you to attack the American. Ramon has brought this on himself.'

Madalena ran from the house, her eyes staring with horror at the scene. On her knees, she cupped Ramon's face in her hands.

'No!' she sobbed. 'Why?'

Steve jerked the mule's head around, but paused in the saddle to look at her. Madalena stared back at him, her eyes clouded with tears.

'You murderer!' she screamed.

Steve braced himself, pursing his lips, but did not reply. He merely nodded quietly in assent, turned the mule around and headed back towards the river, followed by his wolfhound. Any second he expected to feel a bullet ploughing through his back. He was not sure whether he would have cared.

# 5

Peeling paintwork of the Silver Garter reflected the township's past glories. Dancing girls, kicking up their begartered knees in frills and furbelows across the wide false front of pine boards, once enticed a queue of miners to come inside. Now the artistry was faded and hardly discernible. And inside, the scene was but an echo of the past decades when Spanish and Anglos had dug precious metals out of the surrounding hillsides and Silver City had been a boomtown.

The long mahogany bar, with its brass footrail, still remained, but there weren't many bottles on its mirrored shelves behind, nor many customers kicking their heels in the spacious interior. The roulette-table that had once spun night and day, Sundays included, lay idle. The three-legged chairs and battered tables showed evidence of innumerable bar brawls. The floorboards and walls were pocked with bullet holes. An aged professor of the ivories, George Jinks, who had seen it all, desultorily tinkled an out-of-tune piano on a podium, but his fellow musicians had fled. A sprinkling of storekeepers and country jakes talked shop as they took their noon aperitif at the bar. But of the flock of good time girls, who had once serviced a host of randy gold-panners, most had departed for more profitable spots. Only two remained, swinging their legs lethargically from bar stools at one end of the room.

Joan Grigson — or Groaning Joan as she was more commonly known — scratched an itch beneath her left breast and hitched the droopy appendage up more securely in her flimsy lace dress.

'I don't like the look of them jaspers,' she murmured, flicking her cigarette in the direction of the only card-players, a hard-faced bunch hunched over a table in one corner. 'They strike me like rats peering outa their hole just waiting to pounce with their ravenous teeth.'

Honolulu Sal, a stout, half-breed, Spanish-Mescalero Apache, and as such not wanted by either tribe, just shrugged. 'They ain't doin' no harm.' The closest Sal had been to Honolulu was Sante Fe, but she had chosen the name at random for its romantic association, and she did bear some resemblance to an Hawaii islander with her oval face and black hair.

'Not yet they ain't,' Joan replied, letting the cigarette hang from her limp-wristed grasp as she leaned on the bar. 'Maybe we should apprise the sheriff of their presence.'

'Aw, he'll still be sleepin' off his hangover. You see him hit the juice last night?'

'I was with him, dumbcluck. And I had my bit, too. The sheriff and I share problems of an emotional nature in our past. In his cups he's inclined to confide in me.' Groaning Joan pressed an ice-cooled glass of beer to her forehead. 'My head ain't so good, neither.'

'Never mix business with pleasure,' Sal lectured her. 'That leads to a gal's downfall.'

'Heck!' Joan squawked. 'We couldn't fall much lower than we have. Anyway, far as Steve's concerned, it was neither business nor pleasure, just two amigos gittin' drunk.'

The scrawny hostess gave a scowl of displeasure, for she wished that it was not so. She had long harboured a smouldering passion within her skinny frame for the handsome young sheriff. No spring chicken herself, she would often fondly run her fingers through McCormack's blond crop, give him the come-on, but, although always pleasant in his manner to her, he appeared immune to her charms. 'Sometimes I think the sheriff lacks passionate parts. Maybe they were blown off in a gunfight? I'll have to ask him.'

'He's just a deadbeat an' a drunk.

You won't git no cash nor no joy outa him, gal.' Honolulu was more prosaic in her approach to men. She had learned to see them as marks to be sucked dry.

'It ain't his cash I'm after, it's his body. But all I git is his mind. I could do with a little joy.'

'I tol' you,' Sal frowned, 'that ain't no way to approach this profession.'

'Profession? Is that what you call it? A waitress who fucks would be more precise.' Grigson had been a school-marm and her once flowery manner of speech had, since her sojourn in the Silver Garter, become peppered with more earthy expletives. She had been expelled from her job for seducing a fourteen-year-old pupil, although they had both claimed to be in love. Her reputation had followed her and she had been unable to find employment suited to her intelligence. Joan had a strong sex drive and a natural contempt for most men in those parts, so she had drifted into the hostess game. At least it paid better than teaching. Or it had in boomtown days. Pickings lately had been slim.

'Steve's different,' she sighed. 'He's been around. He's a man I can talk to. Sure, he's drinkin' himself to death. But for me that cynical disillusion kinda adds to his allure.'

'Oh, Chrissakes!' Sal groaned. 'Look who the cat brought in. Trouble!'

Kid Waterson leaned on the slatted batwing doors, his upturned eyes swivelling as he cased the gloomy joint. He lived in fear of Estevan being on the prowl. He pushed the doors apart and stood resplendent in a black-silk shirt fringed with silver, black pants tucked into black-and-silver boots, a high-domed white Stetson shielding his eyes, the buckhorn grip of his Smith & Wesson .44 jutting from a tooled holster slung on his right hip, and tied around his thigh by pigging string to keep it steady. He limped into the long bar-room trying to keep the weight off his still painful gun-shot calf. At the bar he paused, removed the black gloves, and stared for seconds at his knuckles, scarred by Estevan's bullet. It made him wince with fury and reminded him of the reason why he was there.

'Gimme a bottle,' he said.

'Mr Waterson, your daddy,' the black barkeep stuttered, 'he tol' me you only gotta be served one glass.'

'You joking?' The Kid flipped his revolver from its holster, whirled it on one finger and stuck the barrel up the negro's left nostril. 'Gimme a bottle, I said.'

'Yassuh.' The keep carefully extricated himself off the end of the revolver. 'I'se only thinkin' of your good health.'

'Huh.' The Kid bit the cork out of the bottle, spat it away, and upended the bottle to his mouth. His Adam's apple bounced as he took a long glug and he gasped from the shock of the fiery liquid, but also relief. 'It's the O.M.'s health you oughta be thinkin' of, Moses, 'cause I got a feelin' me an' him is goin' to have a fallin' out.'

One of the men in the corner, a surly villain, with a string of convictions behind him, known these days as Abel Crouch, glowered at the Kid from behind his wide-brimmed hat and raised a finger, beckoning him. He didn't have many fingers to play with. The middle two were just stumps that had been shot off.

The Kid gave a crooked grin and sauntered across, the bottle in his hand.

'You the man I sent for — Crouch?'

'Thass me. You must be the dude they call the Kid. Meet the boys.' He jerked his thumb in the direction of his scruffy companions, dressed like cowpunchers but slung with belts of bullets and shooting irons. 'Ephraim, Les, Josh. You don't need to know no other names.'

'What you playing? Monte? I'm a dab hand at that game. Deal me in, boys.'

'You planning on gittin' stinkin' drunk, sonny? You don't impress us in them dandified clothes even if your daddy is a big-shot rancher man. You better put that bottle aside and fergit about the play of the cards 'til we hear your deal.'

'Ach, one bottle ain't nuthin' to me. I can drink any man under the table.'

'Sure.' Sidekick Ephraim, long-legged in tattered batwing chaps, leered. 'You mean a bottle of milk, doncha, babyface? I heerd about you. You're usually flat on your back in the gutter more'n standin' upright.'

Josh and Les joined in his guffaws as the Kid's pale face reddened and he stood unsure whether to shoot them down or call their bluff. No, he needed them. So, he grinned his toothy grin and drawled:

'There's only one way to find that out.'

'Cut the crap,' Crouch snarled. 'We ain't rode all this way from Fort Grant to play games with you. I asked you what's the deal?'

The Kid glanced back at the people at the bar and slid on to a chair opposite them, lowering his voice.

'Just a straightforward bit of rustling.

81

I got two hundred dollars in my pocket. There's fifty for each of you. But we gotta keep this hush-hush.'

'Why so?' Abel glanced, alertly, at his colleagues. 'A spot of rustlin' never bothered us. Doctor the brands, sell the beeves to the military back at Fort Grant. Do we get to keep the profit?'

'No. There won't be no profit. There won't be no sale. That's why I'm offering the four of you fifty each. There's no danger entailed. Do you want it or not?'

Les, a balding former blacksmith, now on the run for a killing, looked puzzled.

'If we don't sell 'em what in tarnation we goin' to do with 'em? Eat 'em?'

'Ah, don't be stupid,' Crouch spat out. 'Let's get this clear. Who are we going to be rustling these from?'

'My father, Old Man Waterson.'

'Your father?' The fourth man, an emaciated runt called Josh Smith, who preferred opium to alcohol, almost exploded. 'Are you crazy?'

'Shush,' the Kid hissed. 'Keep it down. Don't tell the whole town. Yeah, the O.M., he can afford to lose a couple hundred head. And I know the perfect spot along by the river miles from the ranch house. There's only a couple punk cowpokes guarding 'em. Schoolboys could do this job.'

'So what then?' Crouch asked. 'Who do we deliver 'em to?'

'Estevan Ramirez. Only he ain't gonna know it — yet. All you gotta do is take 'em across our river, drive them up the scarp through the Burro mountains until you hit the river the Ramirez family owns. You can get there overnight.'

'So what do we do with them then?' Les asked, still at a loss, scratching his head.

'You just send 'em on their way. If you see any of the Ramirez *vaqueros* just leave 'em and get out of it. Go back to where you came from. Fifty dollars for a night's work ain't bad, is it? It takes most 'punchers a month an' a half to earn that.'

'So where will you be,' Crouch asked, 'while this is going on?'

'Back here in town, living it up. I need an alibi. First, this afternoon, I'll show you where the beeves are. Then it's up to you while I get back here fast. Are you interested or should I look for somebody else?'

'Yeah, we'll do it,' Crouch grinned. 'But why give 'em to the Ramirez bunch?'

'Because,' the Kid said, emphatically, 'my daddy's a yellow-bellied louse. He's just a big mouth, him and what he did in the war. I've begged him to go wipe out that nest of rats, the Ramirezes. But he won't. He don't want a war with those filthy greasers, a war we could win easy. He's shit-scared. This way he'll have no option when he finds his cows on their land.'

'Whoo-wee!' Crouch gave a low whistle and tugged at his heavy moustache. 'You're an evil li'l bastard, I gotta hand it to you.'

'Yeah, I am.' The Kid stared at him, fanatically. 'And let me remind you boys, if you try to double-cross me, if you don't leave those beeves on Ramirez land, if you try to drive 'em back to Fort Grant I'll be leading the killing-party that come after you.'

Abel Crouch's sullen face broke into an unaccustomed grin. 'We wouldn't cross you, Kid. The thought never entered our minds. A deal's a deal.' He thrust out his hand to grasp the Kid's. 'Two hundred's fine for our trouble. So let's go take a look-see at this herd an' we'll strike soon as it's sundown.'

'Yeah, right.' The Kid smiled and got to his feet, pleased that his ingenious plan was being put into practice. 'You boys go out first and I'll meet you in half an hour outside town in Bantry Bottom by the old mine. OK? We don't want to rouse any suspicion.'

'Sure.' Abel Crouch rose, too, and jerked his head at his boys. 'Come on, let's do as the man says.'

The Kid watched them leave the saloon, took another swig of the bottle and swaggered over to Joan and Honolulu Sal, saying in a loud voice, 'A nice bunch of fellas, those. Just passing through. They gotta get back to Camp Grant.'

'They didn't look so nice to me,' Joan replied, off-handedly, hitching up her dress again.

'Hey, you look mighty sweet today, Joan.' The Kid's whiskey breath hazed over her as he grabbed her waist and tried to kiss her painted lips. 'How about you and me go out back for a half-hour?'

Joan yelped as he squeezed her bony buttock, and screeched, 'I wouldn't go with you if you was the last punter in Paradise. Get away from me. Don't anybody here know how to treat a lady?'

The men in the bar guffawed as the Kid pushed her from her bar stool, wrestled her and tried to get a hand up her skirt, pulling it high, revealing her none-too-clean pantalettes.

'Yee-ha! Who ya think you are, sister? You ain't nuthin' but some worn-out hoo-er.'

He had placed his bottle on the bar counter while he molested her. Joan's fingers felt for it, picked it up while she struggled with him, and brought it down to smash upon his cranium. The Kid went down on his knees, spluttering.

'Just keep your filthy hands off me,' she screamed.

'Come on, honey.' Honolulu Sal helped him up. 'I'll look after ya. Let's go lie down, do jig-a-jig. Joan ain't no good to ya. She's a disgrace to our noble profession.'

'If she weren't a woman . . . ' The Kid scowled as he brushed glass from his shirt and, an arm around Sal, was helped to the back rooms. 'I'd friggin' kill her.'

'That boy makes my skin crawl,' Joan said, with a shudder, as she straightened her dress. 'Anybody but *him*.'

She turned to the watching men and spread her fingers. '*Anybody?* It's only two dollars.'

The men laughed and turned back to their drinking.

'Let us know when you're down to fifty cents,' the local butcher called. 'I might think about it.'

'Go to hell all of you,' she replied, as she got back on her bar stool. 'What's a lady of my refinement doing in this rat-hole.'

★  ★  ★

Sheriff Steve McCormack locked the iron-studded oaken door of his jail-house and, giving a whistle to Jock, strolled along the dirt-rutted main street of Silver City, past the two-storey brick buildings of the bank and clothing emporium, indicators of more prosperous times, Charley Chung's Chinese laundry, steam pumping from its tin chimney, Joe Oliver's meat market and butcher's shop, the billiards hall and cigar-store, Sadie Thomas's dress parlour, past a blacksmith's livery from which loud clanging sounds emanated, past a wagon being loaded with sacks of flour and grain, and Morrill's opera house where Henry Antrim once sang and danced with the local thespians. He had been known as a pretty good singer, had Billy the Kid.

It was in Silver City that Henry, as he was then known, had taken his first teenage, tentative steps into crime under the influence of Sombrero Jack. He had been indicted for the somewhat absurd theft of clothing from the Chinese laundry and thrown in the sheriff's own jail. But the slim, buck-toothed boy had demonstrated his knack of escapology which saved him, subsequently, several times and, after going up the chimney, had skinned it out of town. He had quickly become horse-thief, rustler and hitman and by the time he was twenty-one had, it was claimed, killed twenty-one men. It was then that he, under his new name,

William Bonney, died by the gun.

Maybe it was the exploits of Billy, much-vaunted in the nation's dime magazines, which had inspired others to emulate him like the dim-brained Kid Waterson who seemed bent on going to hell before his time.

Outside the Silver Garter four strangers were jerking tight the cinches of their mustangs prior to mounting up. Heavily armed, they had that surly air that spoke one word: trouble. Steve jumped up on to the sidewalk and, tipping back his hat to hang by its cord on his back, watched them suspiciously.

'Do I know you fellas?' he asked. 'I got a feeling I seen you someplace.'

Abel Crouch sat in his saddle, his mouth masked by his moustache, his eyes shaded from the noonday sun by his wide-brimmed hat.

'Who the hell are you?'

Steve touched his metal star pinned to his shirt. 'It's my job to look after this town.'

'Heck,' Les giggled, 'jest look at the

tinhorn sheriff. What's it to him who we are?'

'Thass OK,' Abel muttered, 'the sheriff's only doing his job.' He wore a baggy duster coat over his crumpled suit, a gunbelt tight around his waist. 'We just been gargling our throats and waterin' our hosses, is that a crime, mister?'

'Where you from?'

'Here, there and everywhere,' Les grinned. 'Don't wet your pants, Sheriff. We're jest passing through.'

'What business are you men engaged in?'

'Horse-dealing,' Abel replied, 'if it's any business of yours?'

'You're mightily heavily armed for horse-dealers.'

'These are dangerous parts.' Abel spat in the dust and tugged his mustang away. 'So long, Sheriff. You no need to bother about us.'

The three others followed him at an amble down the street, then pricked in their spurs and headed fast out of town.

'Good riddance to bad rubbish in that case,' Steve muttered and turned to enter the saloon.

It was dim and musty inside, smelling of alcohol and tobacco and, as he approached Joan Grigson, cheap perfume.

'Howdy Joan, how's things?'

'Howdy, Steve. How's your head?'

'How's yours?'

Without being asked the negro barkeep had placed before him his morning reviver, a tumbler of rye whiskey and a glass of Kansas steam beer containing a chunk of ice.

'That crew who just left — they caused any trouble?' Steve asked him.

'Good as gold,' the 'keep replied. 'Just sat in the corner playing a hand or two.'

'The Kid was talking to them,' Joan said, in a lowered voice. 'They had their heads together over something. Then they got up and left. He said he knew them from Camp Grant.'

'Waal,' Steve drawled, 'there's a lot of

hobos and no-goods hang around the saloons that cater for the soldiers over there. Horse-thievery's rife. Luckily it's over the Arizona border, out of my jurisdiction. So, the Kid was here, was he?'

'He still is,' Joan grinned. 'He's back there sampling the erotic delights of Honolulu Sal. When you gonna give me a try, Sheriff?'

'Ach, well, I'll have to think about it.' He patted her stockinged leg revealed by her split dress, and swallowed the whiskey in two gulps, shaking his head and wincing. 'I'm sorry to tell you I got a bad crush on a Latino gal at the moment. Maybe I'll get over her. There don't seem much future in it.'

'Maybe I could help you forget her, Steve?' It was Joan's turn to let her fingers play across his knee. 'Why you wanna waste time thinkin' about someone you can't have? You know I'm always ready and waiting.'

'Ai, yeah,' he sighed, sipping at the iced beer as the whiskey glowed through him. 'Why ruin a good friendship, Joan?'

'I could always give up this lousy profession if you wanted me — '

'I wish you would, Joan. You *could* get out. You *could* get a job in a store. There's plenty of men looking for a wife.'

'What,' she snorted, scornfully, 'these corn-sucking hicks around here?'

'Look Joan, I got a lot of paperwork to do. I gotta take a look through the back numbers of the *Police Gazette*. I reckon that's where I seen the mug-shots of one of them *hombres*.' He finished his beer, winked at her, and headed for the door. 'Might see you later.'

'Sheriff,' Joan called, 'if you're thinking of going after those four you'd better watch your back.'

Without turning he pointed his finger like a pistol at the ceiling and pushed through the batwing doors. What, he wondered, could the Kid have been discussing with them?

He stopped off at Frank Whiley's gunshop to buy a box of .44s and Frank invited him to step outside and try out a big new Magnum .357 just come in. Out in Whiley's backyard target area Steve caught sight of the Kid getting on his piebald at the back of the Silver Garter saloon and heading fast away from the town. There was something furtive about his leaving as if he didn't want to be seen.

'Where's he sneakin' off to?' he muttered. 'He ain't gittin' pie-eyed today. He must be up to something.'

Frank grinned. 'Maybe daddy's insisted that he gets home afore sundown.'

'That, my friend, ain't very likely.'

But what concern was it of his? It made a pleasant change that the Kid wasn't up to his usual stupid tricks, shouting and swearing, shooting out street lights, lassoing respectable ladies, or riding his horse into the emporium and causing a hell of a mess.

'Jeez, this has got a kick to it.' He fired the Magnum at the target. 'You need a strong wrist.'

'Them slugs will go right through a man at fifty feet.'

'Yeah, and probably an innocent bystander behind him.' The Magnum roared as he emptied the cylinder. 'I'll stick to my Peacemaker, Frank.'

When he unlocked his jailhouse he wondered, again, about the Kid. He had had to lock him up on several occasions. His big fat mama generally arrived to bail him out and pay his fine.

'Aw, he ain't worth bothering about,' he said to Jock.

# 6

'Why wait for sundown,' Abel Crouch snarled, as he sat his horse and watched the herd of longhorns peacefully grazing along the riverbank. 'Let's take 'em now.'

'That's not a good idea . . . ' the Kid began. He and his four rustlers were concealed in the overhanging branches of a grove of willows, its leaves gracefully dancing upon the stream. But he was ignored.

'Hup! Hi! H'yah!' Crouch shouted, as he whipped his mustang with his reins and went splashing across the river from the south bank to the north bank, followed by his *compadres*, who were also hooting and hollering. They reached solid ground and fanned out behind the herd of some 200 cows, calves and bulls, setting them jumping forward in a startled run, bellowing their surprise and annoyance. With expertise the rustlers cracked their lariats, flapped their hats, and sent the beasts running in a semicircle back towards the river.

The Kid watched, biting his lips anxiously, from the shade of the trees, unwilling to be seen by any of his father's men. There were only two young punchers taking their ease, lounging by their fire on the bank of the river. He knew them only by their first names, Roy and Jimmy — he didn't pay much heed to hired staff. They jumped up as the four *pistoleros* came swinging in to the attack. Roy went running across, waving his arms, panicking, futilely trying to stop the charge of the thundering longhorns.

'The durn idjit,' the Kid yelped, as he saw Roy gored and trampled underfoot. There was a sharp scream as the rest of the herd surged on over him and splashed across the river to the southern bank.

The other drover, Jimmy, had thrown

up his hands and backed away to his fire as he watched the four hard riders cut out the herd. Their mustangs kicked up clods of earth as they charged past him.

'Where the hell you come from?' Jimmy stuttered, as the leading rider in a billowing duster coat watched the herd cross the river, then swung his mount around and cantered back. He had a sawn-off 8-gauge in one fist. 'It ain't no skin off my nose, mister. I cain't stop ya, can I?' Jimmy backed further away and tripped into the fire, kicking and scrabbling away from the horse's hooves and the dark presence of the mounted man hovering over him. 'You can have 'em. Please! No, mister!'

The boy cried out in fear and agony as first one barrel and then the second flowered flame, exploding shot into him, cutting his insides apart. 'No . . . ohhhh.'

His last word trailed off as blood spurted from numerous large ventilations and he expired. Abel Crouch looked down at him, his eyes and mouth expressionless, only making sure that he was dead. Then he turned his horse and rode after the others.

'What are you doing?' the Kid demanded of him in a voice pitched high with fear. 'I didn't tell you to kill 'em.'

Crouch took two cartridges from his coat pocket, pressed them into the shotgun's barrel, snapped it shut and pointed it the Kid's way.

'Dead men tell no tales,' he said, with a humourless grin. 'Maybe I should do the same to you?'

The Kid whipped out his fancy Smith & Wesson and held it outstretched, aimed at Crouch's chest, even though his hand was shaking.

'You try cocking that piece I'll have you first. This is a double action. I'm warning you.'

'Ha!' Abel Crouch gave a gasping laugh, and lowered the 8-gauge. 'I'm only kidding. That sceered ya didn't it, Kid? You got any more easy jobs like this you want done, you let me know. Next time you pay me, private-like. The boys don't need to know the score.'

The Kid kept his revolver trained on Crouch, watching as the three men chasing the herd disappeared over the prow of a hill in their cloud of dust.

'You make sure you do what we agreed and leave those beeves on the greasers' land. Otherwise there'll be a reckoning.'

'Sure,' Crouch cackled. 'You frighten me.' He jerked his mustang's head away and went pounding off to follow the others in their dust-haze.

'Shoot!' The Kid wiped a sweat of fear from his eyes and nose and went to look at the mangled remains of Roy and the bloody body of Jimmy. 'Poor bastards!'

He looked around him anxiously at the wooded hillsides, at the skyline. 'I better git outa here.'

The Kid spurred his horse away, galloping hard back towards Silver City. 'Hot damn,' he shouted. 'All I gotta do now is face Pa.' His heart pounded to the tattoo of the hoofs as he imagined his father's wrath and wondered, bitterly, why his carefully thought-out plan had begun to go haywire.

★ ★ ★

Madalena Ramirez's pale face was severe and determined as she took the sharp knife and traced an incision around the hole where her brother Ramon had been shot, watched the blood seep. She parted the skin with her fingers and cut deeper. There was a muffled scream from her brother, but he had been dosed with mescal and was high as a kite. Emilio hung on to his legs as he tossed and twitched, while Estevan sat on his head, trying to hold him still.

'Bring the light closer, Father,' she ordered.

She had no real knowledge of anatomy or medicine, apart from what she had read out of curiosity, but she could see that the bullet had penetrated three inches or so beneath the appendix region and Ramon was haemorrhaging internally. It was an area of tender veins and nerves. She gritted her teeth as Ramon writhed and screamed more shrilly.

'Hold him still,' she hissed, and probed further.

Madalena had come across the leather case of surgical instruments in a pawnshop in Santa Fe and had bought them on impulse. They had been hocked, the pawnbroker said, by a doctor called Holliday. He needed cash to buy medicine, meaning alcohol. The slim scalpel certainly did an expert job.

'There it is,' she breathed out. 'Give me the tweezers.'

Her maid, Rosa, dipped the tweezers in her bowl of boiling water and passed them over. Madalena took them and delicately probed the bleeding wound as her father held a hurricane lamp overhead and watched, transfixed, as did the others.

'Got it!' Madalena produced the bullet with a hiss of triumph. 'It was lodged against the hipbone. The bone appears to be intact.'

She had carbolized everything after taking the decision to operate, her hands, the sponges, swabs, scalpels, and the table Ramon lay on.

'Right, Rosa, I want you to pour that water into him. Flush him right out. Use all of the two gallons. With any luck it will stop the internal bleeding.'

Madalena sat back, wiped a stray strand of hair from her forehead, and watched her maid perform the task.

'Now,' she said, 'all I have to do is sew him up again.'

She tried to relax as she washed the blood from her hands and shook her fingers dry before commencing the suture. When she was finished she gave a gasp of relief. 'Now all we can do is pray,' she said, crossing herself.

'Will he pull through?' Estevan asked.

'I'm afraid the shock will be too much for him.'

'He's as tough as an ox,' the old man muttered. 'He's a Ramirez. He'll make it.'

* * *

Sheriff McCormack was doing a two-finger exercise on a big Remington typewriter, the newfangled addition to a lawman's armoury. He bit his lower lip as he concentrated to write his report on the attack on him by Ramon Ramirez and why he had been forced to reply as a matter of self-preservation. He tried to keep it brief, just sticking to the facts. It would have to be submitted to the town council, who would send it back to the authorities in Santa Fe. He added that in the event of Ramon's death an inquest would be held. He ripped the page out from the roller, lounged back in his padded swivel-chair, put his boots up on his desk, and sucked at a pencil as he studied it. 'Hmm, OK. That's what happened, ain't it?' he asked his dog. The hound blinked his agreement.

Steve popped the folded report into one of the desk's pigeonholes and looked around him. Not much of a place to call home. The bare adobe walls, the net on the ceiling to catch tarantulas and centipedes, the oak door, beneath which dust blew in from off the street, the barred window, the large barred cell, an iron pot-belly stove, his coffee-pot and frying-pan, an oilskin-covered table and a chair, a pile of law-books on the floor, notices of wanted criminals and old *Police Gazettes*. He picked up one of these magazines in which he had found the following notice:

Herb Sontag, escaped from Colorado state penitentiary, white man, thick-set, age 34, six ft. two ins., brown hair, thick moustache, sallow complexion, brown eyes, two middle fingers of right hand missing, serving five years for armed robbery. Previous convictions for arson, rape, forgery, buggery, horse-theft, larceny, drunkenness, disturbing the peace and rustling. A reward of $500 will be paid for his capture alive and return.

What had caught the sheriff's attention was the daguerreotype likeness: it had all the attributes of the hard-faced *hombre* who had appeared to be leader of the 'horse dealers' outside the Silver Garter that afternoon.

'Maybe we oughta git after him,' he muttered. 'Five hundred dollars would come in handy.'

But he couldn't be certain. He hadn't noticed anything amiss with his hand. But he had been wearing gloves. The rest fitted. 'Is it worth bothering?' he wondered. 'He ain't caused me any trouble. I cain't go chasin' after every desperado who drifts through.'

He went out to the privy, which backed on to the big ditch which had been dug by the council to carry run-off from mountain storms around the town and who should he see riding back along it but the Kid? Why was he leaving and returning in such an evasive manner instead of by the main thoroughfare? He watched him climb his piebald up the bank and ride to the back door of the Silver Garter.

'Funny,' the sheriff said. 'C'mon, Jock, we better take a look.'

The piebald was blowing hard, his flanks streaming sweat, his hoofs caked with red mud, possibly river mud. That was the direction he had come from, the Okinotchie river, which snaked through the Waterson grasslands.

Steve went through the back door of the saloon and found Honolulu Sal in one of the small rooms, sat on a crumpled bed, plucking at her eyebrows before a cracked glass.

'Howdy, Honolulu. How's it going? You had any customers this afternoon?'

'Oh, yeah, Sheriff.' Her eyes swivelled towards him. 'I been wid the Kid for two hours. From two pee em to now. He just gone back into bar.'

'Two hours. That's a long session for any man.'

'He fell asleep, thass why. But when he woke he paid me for the whole time. He is a good kid.'

'Yeah? You think so? Would you mind coming with me into the bar? I just want to ask him a few questions.'

'Sure, I'll come. Just let me get my slippers on.'

The Kid was standing by the bar, a bottle of whiskey in his hand, bragging volubly about what a great time he'd been having with Honolulu Sal for the past two hours when Steve stepped up behind him and slid his Smith & Wesson out of his holster.

'Hey!' The Kid spun on him, his face livid. 'What the hell you doing? No man takes my guns.'

'Looks like I have.' The sheriff turned the cylinder, sniffed at the barrel. 'And it looks like you ain't used this lately. That's somethang in your favour.'

'So damn what? Give me my gun.'

Steve stuffed the S. & W. in his own

belt. 'Why don't you try to take it, you jumped-up li'l mama's boy.'

'Fugg you!' The Kid smashed the bottle on the counter and thrust it wildly at McCormack's face. But the sheriff was ready for him. He ducked to one side, grabbed the Kid's arm, twisted it behind his back and chopped him across the side of the jaw with the side of his fist. 'Aagh!' the Kid cried, as he went down.

The sheriff took steel cuffs from his belt, put a boot on the youth's back, holding him down, and locked first one wrist and then the other.

'What the hell you doing?' the Kid screamed.

'I'm arresting you for an attempted assault with a deadly weapon on a peace officer.'

'You damn well asked for it. I'll have your job for this. My daddy runs this town.'

'You think so?' Steve dragged the Kid to his feet. 'So why you trying to put up this fake alibi? What you been doing along the river? You and those ugly-looking pals of yours.'

'What?' the Kid spluttered. 'What you on about? I been with Sal all afternoon. Ain't that right, Sal?'

'Sure, he with me, jig-a-jig, two hours.'

'Don't give me that crap, you lyin' li'l two-bit whore.' Steve pointed a finger at her. 'Or I'll arrest you, too.'

'Hey,' Groaning Joan butted in. 'Don't talk to Sal like that.'

'Keep out of this, Joan. I just seen him sneak in the back of town. His horse is all steamed up. Naturally, a runt like him wouldn't bother giving it a rub down. He's in too much of a hurry to try to make out he's been here all afternoon.'

'There's still no need to call Sal names,' Joan protested, shrilly. 'You call her that you're including me.'

'I call a spade a spade, Joan. That's what you both are, ain't it — prostitutes? I oughta arrest you both.'

'Don't make me laugh,' the Kid

jeered. 'The O.M. owns this saloon.'

'Yeah. Maybe I should indict him, too, for pimping.' But he could not help smiling, himself, as the other men in the saloon roared with laughter at the absurdity of such an idea.

'Anyhow,' he said, grabbing the Kid by his throat, 'all I want to know is what's going on.' He squeezed the Kid's windpipe with his left hand and his right fist jabbed in hard to the Kid's solar plexus, going in deep. The Kid went down on one knee, coughing, choking and groaning. 'You wanna lose your looks, pretty boy?' He booted him in the jaw and sent him slithering back across the floor. 'Or you wanna talk?'

'Steve!' Joan caught hold of the sheriff's arm as he tensed it ready for another blow. 'This ain't right. Leave him be.'

'Keep out of this, Joan. Or I'll lock you up, too.'

'You what? You lousy bully. This is a breach of his rights. Leave him alone.'

For reply Steve jerked the Kid's face

up close and smacked his open hand viciously back and forth twice across his jaws, making his head snap from side to side. He clenched his fist and thrust it in the Kid's face.

'Talk, you piece of crap,' he roared. 'Or do you want more? You're gonna talk if I have to beat you to pulp.'

'No!' the youth screamed. 'Don't! It's nothing to do with me. I didn't do anything. It was them.'

'What you saying? What did they do?'

'They shot him. They killed him, Jimmy, one of the O.M.'s boys.' The Kid was almost hysterical, snot and blood trickling from his nose. 'I didn't tell them to. I just told them to rustle a few cows.'

'To rustle a few of your old man's cows? What the hell for?'

'To make it look like it was Estevan,' the Kid cried.

'Ah, I see.' Steve threw him aside. 'So which of 'em did the shooting?'

'The older one. Crouch. The one with the moustache.'

'The one who's got two of his fingers missing?'

'Yeah, he has. He used a sawn-off.' The Kid hung to the bar, whimpering. 'He did it for no reason. I couldn't stop him, Sheriff. I'm telling you the truth. I don't want to hang.'

'You tell me the truth, I'll protect you, Caleb. Give him a whiskey fer Chrissakes. You better give me one, too.'

Joan watched as the barkeep put a glass of red-eye to the Kid's puffed lips, then slid another along to the sheriff; she watched Steve grip the bar with one hand and take a steady slug of the potato lightning.

'There's sure a side of you I never knew about,' she marvelled. 'I allus thought you were a nice guy.'

'Sometimes there's only one way of making a punk like him talk,' he gritted out. 'Give him a good thrashing. I guess he's never had one afore, more's the pity.'

'So, what are you going to do now?'

'I'm going after them, what do you think?'

'But there's four of them. Hard men. There's only one of you. Aren't you going to raise a posse?'

'Ha! You joking? I figure I'll do better on my own. First I gotta put the Kid in the hoosegow for his own protection — from his father.' He tossed back the rest of the whiskey with a grimace. 'Then I gotta git goin' fast as I can 'fore sundown.'

He turned and gave her a flicker of a smile. 'I didn't mean what I said about cha. You ain't *really* a prostitute. Your heart ain't in it.'

She gave him a grin. 'It was the two-bit bit that hurt.' She watched him give the Kid a push and lead him to the door and called out, 'Steve, be careful.'

# 7

'You gonna have plenty time to git used to this cell, boy,' the sheriff drawled, as he shoved the Kid into the barred 'slammer' and removed his handcuffs. 'You ain't gonna git out until I get back, that's if I do. Still, it will give you an idea of what your home will be like for the next thirty years the way you're going. You better sit here and think about that.'

'Aw, get lost. My Ma'll have me out soon as she hears about this.' The Kid touched his aching jaw and still-stinging cheek. 'It's you who's gonna end up in the hoosegow. We'll arraign you for brutality to a suspect, deprivation of a prisoner's rights, eliciting a forced confession under duress, and damaging my teeth.'

'Oh, my! Which sharpjack lawyer you been talking to? You really scare me,

Kid.' Steve slammed the door to and locked it, peering into the cage as if to satisfy himself that there was no way out. The floor was made of river-sand, bullock's blood and cactus-juice which hardened like cement. The walls were four feet thick, solid adobe. The thick iron bars of the open front were sunk deep into the ground, unshakeable. He gave them a tug, just to make sure. Not a tremor. '*Adios*.'

'Hey, you can't just walk out and leave me,' the Kid hollered. 'What about my supper?'

'Oh, yeah.' Steve picked up a piece of cornbread and the remains of a side of bacon from his own supper the night before, which were still on his table. He tossed them through the bars. 'Here. Don't eat it all at once. It may have to last you a few days. Too good for him, ain't it, Jock? C'mon, boy, let's go.'

'Hey,' the Kid wailed, 'you can't just leave me.'

'The bucket with water in's for drinking. The other bucket to piss in or whatever. You can't say we don't cater for your needs.'

The sheriff took his rifle from the rack and stepped outside with the huge hound. 'That oughta make him think,' he said, as he locked the oak door.

The mule was in his stable giving vent to an agonized bray about his forced inactivity.

'Doncha worry, ol' Moose, you'll be prayin' for me to stop soon enough.' He slung his saddle-bags over him behind the cantle. He had packed another hunk of bacon and cornbread, with hard tack and pemmican, to last a few days, his toothbrush, razor, and two boxes of ammunition. As an afterthought he had carefully added four sticks of dynamite, which he had been planning to try out one of these days to see what their effect was. They might come in handy. He grabbed hold of the pommel and swung aboard, guiding the mule out and down through the narrow main street. Moose had his head up and was still braying, but more proudly now.

Steve pulled in beside an adobe shack, one of a whitewashed row on the outside of town. The population of Silver City, some 400 souls, was mainly Anglo, but there were a few Latinos and this was their quarter. Epitacio Luna, as he was quaintly called, opened his wooden, ill-fitting door, his dark face splitting into a smile beneath his chock of grey hair when he saw the sheriff.

'Buenos dias, jefe,' he called. 'You going for a ride?'

'Yeah, can you watch the shop?'

'Sure.' The elderly Epitacio had been a lawman of sorts in his time but was badly hogtied by the arthritics these days. He was all the town council would run to by the way of helping Steve to patrol his 10,000 square acres that comprised the Silver City and environs jurisdiction.

'I got a prisoner in the poke. Leave him to stew on his own 'til the morning. Give him some grub but keep him cooped up. Watch out for him, pal.

He's as vicious as a bag of rats.'

'Who is he?'

'Kid Waterson.'

'Him,' Señor Luna sneered. 'I ain't worried about him.'

'His mama and papa may turn up demanding he gets bail bond. You tell 'em to go see the judge afore you let him out. Savvy?'

'Sí, Steve, I savvy. I am not born yesterday.'

'Right. Keep your carbine handy, old-timer, 'case anybody tries to bust him out.' He kicked Moose into action. 'So long.'

He was like a coiled spring. He needed to ride hard and fast along the river to get to the dead cowboy before Old Man Waterson did. He needed to stop a feud developing into a bloody battle. But he had forced himself to unwind, make sure everything was in order before he rode out. A lawman needed to act logically, with due caution, if he was to stay alive or even keep his job.

Fools rush in ... was one of the better maxims.

*  *  *

Steve rounded a bend of the Okinotchie River at a jogtrot, about the best the mule could do by way of a gallop, but a good enough lope, sure enough. There were the deep tracks in the red mud of the cloven-footed herd who had recently been rushed across, with the prints of iron-shod hoofs mingled among them.

'There he is,' he said, spying the body of Jimmy, the young cowpuncher on the ground on the far bank.

He went splashing across followed by the wolfhound and stared down at the corpse. There were great holes an inch across in the boy's chest from which his life-blood had poured.

'Chrissakes! He musta used a goose-gun on him. A double-barrel eight gauge.'

His blood froze cold, in spite of the

heat, when he cast about and found the torn remains in the mud of the cowboy's *compadre*, Roy. He was hardly recognizable as a human after the stampede of longhorns had trodden him into the ground.

'Jeez,' he whispered. 'How the hell am I s'posed to take his body in?'

There was a ominous thundering of the ground, but this stampede was led by Old Man Waterson, who came thudding across the grassland towards him, followed by a bevy of riders. They drew up in a cloud of dust beside the sheriff.

'Is he dead?' Waterson shouted, as he looked down at Roy.

'Waal,' Steve said, grimly, 'he ain't gittin' any older. What the hell you think?'

'Come on. Look at them tracks,' James Waterson cried. 'They're headin' due south. The Ramirez boys did this.'

'Wait a minute,' Steve shouted. 'It weren't the Ramirez. It was . . . '

But Waterson wasn't waiting to hear

any explanations. He had raised his hand and led his men charging forward across the river, churning through it and up the bank on the south side. 'It was your son . . . ' Steve's words faded out, ineffectually, unheard. 'Aw, shee-it. What am I doing? I shoulda grabbed him by the shirt an' talked some sense into him. Now we gotta chase after 'em 'fore we git a bloodbath on our hands.'

That was easier said than done. The cowhands on their wiry and fiery mustangs could go a lot faster than a mule. And there was a long way to go before they reached the Ramirez river.

'C'mon, Moose,' Steve yelled, slapping the beast's sides with his lariat, 'cain't you go no faster? We're losing 'em.' The sheriff knew, however, that if he pushed Moose too hard he would soon be flogging a dead mule. So he relaxed and let him go at a steady lope.

The great fiery ball of the sun was sinking, flushing the sky roseate and time was fast running out. Steve's heart, too, seemed to sink as he heard the rattle of small-arms fire in the near distance, echoing through the canyons. 'Sounds like they're already at each other's throats,' he grunted, as he followed the clear trail of longhorns and horsemen up through a forest of saguaro cactus, their arms reaching at odd angles to the sky. Jock was the first to reach the ridge and he bayed excitedly as Steve on the mule struggled up to join him.

The scene that spread out before him was of the winding Ramirez river in its lush grasslands, with, beyond, the fortified *hacienda*, its adobe walls the colour of burnt ochre in the dying rays of the sun. The opposing factions had settled into cover on either side of the river and were blazing away at each other with revolvers and carbines.

'Blasted fools,' Steve growled. 'How am I goin' to stop 'em?'

It looked as though the initially fierce battle had reached a kind of stalemate and, hopefully, there were as yet no men killed. Blood could only lead to more blood.

Maybe there was a way to make them pay heed to him. Shock tactics! Dynamite! It had been invented by some Swedish scientist, Alfred Nobel, who made the odd claim that it should be used for peaceful purposes. So, perhaps, in this case, it could be. It was a long shot, but there was no way he was going to stop them by merely riding down between the two sides. They would most likely just shoot him from the mule.

The sheriff took one of the dynamite sticks from his saddle-bag, a tin box of matches from his shirt-pocket and, cupping his hands, lit the fuse. It began to sputter and spark.

'Right, I ain't got much time. Stay, Jock. Stay, I said,' he shouted.

The wolfhound watched alertly as his master on his mule went charging down the slope and swerved in along the river bank between the two fighting factions . . .

Explosions were crashing out and bullets whistling past his head. The sheriff ducked low as he rode and began hollering. He went heading right between them. The mule's stiff-legged gait was not rocket-propelled and they could easily have dislodged the rider from his saddle. But, more out of surprise, the gunmen held their fire. It was even more of a surprise when the sheriff hurled the dynamite into the shallow river and there was a huge crash as a plume of water soared. Rocks and mud rained down on both factions.

Steve rode on through the falling rubble and hauled the mule in, standing in the stirrups between the warring sides. He held up a hand as the men fell silent. 'You men, hold your fire. You're warring for no reason. Mr Waterson, the Ramirez boys didn't steal your herd. It was four other *hombres*. The Kid put them up to it.'

'The Kid?' Waterson shouted. 'What the hell you talking about? You mean Caleb?'

' 'Yeah, Caleb. I got him in custody. He's confessed. The hot-headed fool didn't mean for your cowboys to git killed. It was one of them others did it. I got a murder warrant out on him.'

'The Kid?' Old Man Waterson showed himself from behind his rock, carbine in hand. 'I don't believe it. Nobody could be that crazy.'

'It's true,' Steve shouted. 'That boy's an anointed idiot.'

'Keep down, Pa,' Waterson's eldest son, Jed hissed at him. 'Those greasers over there ain't going to quit shooting.'

'Señor Ramirez!' The sheriff yelled over to the Mexican side of the river. 'Order your men to put up their weapons. There's been a mistake. It ain't you we're after.'

'*Madre de Dios!*' Don Luis rose from the cover of the long grass. 'You men come here to attack us and say there has been a mistake? It is a mistake we will rectify.'

'Look, *señor*, Mr Waterson's already lost two men. He mistakenly thought it

127

was your boys did it. Don't let's have any more dead for no reason. Why don't you come forward to the river bank and talk this over?'

'Don't listen to him,' Estevan hissed, cocking his revolver. 'It's a trick. They'll shoot you down like a dog. Those gringos care for nobody. They want us dead.'

'You heard the sheriff, Estevan. There's been a mistake. The Kid is the cause of this.'

'*Sí*, I should have killed him.'

Don Luis kept hold of his carbine but raised one arm as he approached.

'What have you done to my river?' he called out to Steve. 'What the hell caused that explosion?'

'Dynamite. Hey, look there!' Steve grinned as he pointed to dead fish floating on the water, and others flapping on the bank. 'I thought I'd provide you with fresh fish for supper.'

Old Man Waterson, too, walked forward and stooped to pick up a fat trout. 'You carry that stuff with you everywhere? You got any more of it?'

'Coupla sticks. It was like the only way I could get your attention.'

'You saying my son is behind this?'

'Yep. He initiated the rustling. He wanted to provoke you to attack Señor Ramirez. But he enrolled four wild dogs he couldn't control. He says one of them goes by the name of Sontag or Crouch did the killing.'

Waterson, in his curly-brimmed Stetson and wide, leather chaps, savoured this information, then cleared his throat and spat. 'He never was no damned good, that boy. I'm shamed to have spawned him.' He looked across the river at Don Luis. 'I guess I owe you an apology. We got things wrong this time. If it's OK by you we'll round up our longhorns and drive 'em back.'

'That is OK. Take them and go,' Señor Ramirez shouted. 'But don't ever make the mistake of attacking us again. You understand?'

'Sure, I understand.' Waterson turned to Steve. 'You going after those killers?

You need any help?'

'No, I think I can handle 'em.' Steve suddenly caught sight of Madalena riding fast down towards them. She was dressed in a white blouse, a stiff-brimmed hat and riding-skirt, sitting side-saddle. She pulled up in a cloud of dust and spoke to her father then rode forward.

'Howdy,' the sheriff called. 'You look kinda purty. Even purtier than I can recall.'

'I just want to thank you for stopping a bloodbath. And I want to apologize for calling you a murderer. Ramon told me he tried to kill you. You acted in self-defence. And, anyway, he is making a good recovery.'

'Waal,' Steve drawled, 'that's nice to know.'

'Are you going to make a charge against him?'

'Aw, I dunno. I'm still alive, ain't I? Right now, I got other things to think about.'

'Madalena,' her father called sharply.

'That's enough. You've said what you had to say.'

The girl's expressive eyes were dark and doleful in the twilight as she stared hesitantly across the divide between herself and the sheriff. She could easily have splashed across but she feared to upset her father and brothers.

'Goodbye,' she called.

'*Adios, señorita*. Have a nice supper.'

The *vaqueros* had revealed themselves and were leaping about picking up fish. It certainly was going to be a feast. 'Hey, gringo,' one called. 'Lend us some of that dynamite.'

'You better stick to your fishing-rods.' Steve grinned, put two fingers to his mouth and gave a piercing whistle to summon his wolfhound. He rode away to join him, and gave a wave of his hand, without turning in the saddle, as he disappeared into the dusk, heading westerly along the river towards the dark and forbidding razor-sharp mountains of the border.

# 8

Epitacio Luna put his bootheels up on the sheriff's desk and swung back and forth on the swivel-chair. It was early morning and he was enjoying the feeling of being a lawman again. He lit an acrid ten-cent cheroot and blew a smoke ring in the air.

'Hey, old man,' the Kid called. 'How about some grub? You gonna let me starve to death?'

'You'll be dead soon enough, kicking on the end of a rope. Which way would you rather go?' Señor Luna liked his sense of power over the Waterson boy. He had too often seen him drunk and abusing those who couldn't fight back. 'You deserve to die, scumbag. Your daddy's riches won't save you this time.'

'I tol' ya, I didn't kill Jimmy,' the Kid screamed. 'It was Crouch. How could I know he was some crazy psychopath?'

'You may not have pulled the trigger, you white trash. But you set the scene up. The jury ain't gonna have any hesitation in finding you guilty of that poor cowpoke's slaying.'

'No jury would find me guilty. I'm a Waterson.'

'Sure, an' we're all sick of you Watersons throwing your weight about. It's gonna be a pleasure to me to string you up.' Epitacio tugged at his moustache-ends and smiled over at the Kid. 'I've already volunteered my services as hangman.'

The Kid swallowed the bile in his throat. 'Aw, come on,' he wheedled. 'Be a sport. I'm starving. Fry me up some of them eggs an' spuds like you had. My stomach's rumbling.'

'*Sí*, mighty nice snack that was.' The aroma still lingered in the jailhouse. Epitacio had found one of the sheriff's half-finished bottles in a desk drawer and put out a paw to sample the whiskey. 'This is the life, eh, *amigo*?'

'Look, I got cash.' The Kid pulled some crumpled greenbacks from the pocket of his fancy black shirt. 'Ten dollars I'll give ya for breakfast. No, twenty. That's daylight robbery but you can have it. There y'are.'

The old lawman looked across at the bills held out to him through the bars.

'*Sí*, OK, you make an offer I can't refuse.' He swivelled around in his chair, stomped across and snatched the greenbacks. 'You like to-may-toes?' He poked at the stove, splashed olive-oil into the pan, chopped tomatoes, bacon, garlic, red pepper, tossed it into the pan, broke two eggs into it. 'You get good breakfast,' he said, as he swished it around over the flames shooting from the stove-hole. 'You can't say I cheat you.'

'Good.' The Kid's mouth was watering. 'My mama will be here soon to bail me out.'

'Oh, no. I got strict orders to keep everybody out. Not let nobody in. You don' get no bail bond on murder charge.' Epitacio tipped the contents of the frying pan on to a tin plate and sauntered across. 'Don' say I don' do nuthin' for you.'

'You're a good man, Mr Luna.' The Kid eagerly put out his hands to the plate as it was offered him through a letter-box-like aperture in the bar. But, instead of taking the plate, he grabbed the old man's wrists, and hauled his arms through. The plate of food clattered to the floor. He pinned the wrists to his chest with one forearm and reached the other through to snatch at Epitacio's, thick grey hair. He smashed the old-timer's head into the bars, again and again, repeatedly, until he began to slump, unconscious. Then he grabbed at Luna to hold him upright while he released the ring of keys from his belt.

'Gotcha,' he cried in triumph, letting the lawman fall to the floor.

The Kid smiled arrogantly, quickly unlocking the barred gate of his cell, only pausing to scoop some of the spilt food back out of the dust on to the plate. He started stuffing it hungrily into his mouth.

'Mm, you're right,' he spluttered, his mouth full. 'It's a nice breakfast.'

The old man groaned, so he booted him in the gut. 'Shuddup! I don't want a word outa you. Nobody ain't hanging me, mister, 'specially not you.' He found a coil of rope on a hook and hogtied Luna, stuffing a bandanna in his mouth to gag him. His horn-handled Smith & Wesson was hanging above the gun-rack. He buckled it on and took a Marlin rifle, loading it from a box of ammunition. He unlocked the main oak door and peered out. It was early Sunday morning and hardly a soul to be seen.

'So long, sucker,' he sneered at Luna.

He locked up behind him, and went round the back to the stable to find his piebald. He saddled up, pulled his white Stetson down over his brow, filled his canteen at the pump and jumped aboard, setting off at a gallop out of town. It was good to feel free again. He raked the horse's sides with his cruel Mexican spurs. It was a long ride to the border.

★   ★   ★

The sheriff woke with a start from his sleep, jerking up his rifle in readiness. It was broad daylight but there was nobody around. He had ridden most of the night until, exhausted, he had rolled himself in his blanket beneath some bushes hanging over a dry wash and fallen into a deep sleep for a few hours.

He had been dreaming of her again, Irene, the girl he had married. A senseless dream without rhyme or reason. She had been leading him along some street in a city like El Paso, where they had first met. Yes, there were the saloons, the new railroad. But the dream had already become hazy. He remembered her mother was there with them. That old termagant. Why couldn't he forget them?

But, he guessed, if a man married a

woman it was a big step in his life and not easily forgotten. Especially when there was a child involved. It had been just one of those things, two youngsters having fun and going too far. And out of the blue she had told him she was pregnant and her mother had caught him by the arm, twisting it, and had shoved him into their barn.

'I know what you've done to her,' she had hissed. 'You are going to marry her, aren't you?'

Once the initial besottedness with Irene began to fade he realized she wasn't all he had imagined her to be. Sure, even after the child was born, Irene's brand of sexiness still taunted and tantalized him, but there was something brittle and tawdry about her painted face, her jibes at him, her flighty hysterical manner. He tried to hold down a steady, dull-as-ditch-water job to support them. But he had always been wild and it was hard for him. And he was convinced she was coming-on to other men behind his back. Oh, he didn't blame her. He wasn't the ideal husband. He started to drink, to stay out late, playing cards, looking at the girls. He was no angel. But it seemed like he and Irene just had nothing in common any longer.

It was the boy that made him stay. He adored that kid, Jack, as he grew from being a toddler to a sweet-faced youngster. Every day he was different, growing up. They learned together, played together and it was obvious the boy adored him. Irene was more inclined to be sharp and strict, saying he was spoiling him. Steve had taken a job as shotgun on the stage line. He had a good idea what was going on while he was away. There had been a lot of bile, counter-accusations. When he had come home unexpectedly and found a big, burly storekeeper in his marital bed it had all blown up. Yes he had been mad. He had wanted to throttle her, beat the storekeeper to pulp. But what was the use? After a lot of pain and hoohah Irene had taken the boy and moved in with the store-keeper on Santa Fe Street.

It was then that Steve McCormack had hit the trail, drifting like the tumbling tumbleweed out of Texas and into New Mexico. He was gutted by the whole business. He couldn't stay and see his boy living in the house of another man. Occasionally he would pencil a brief note and send a few dollars. She wrote and told him she had got a divorce and would be marrying the storekeeper, Robert Gash. He replied to wish them luck. And moved on. His pain he treated with whiskey. It helped him forget, helped him sleep at night.

Steve sighed as yet again it all came back to him. He looked around for his only pal these days, Jock. He was snuffling at a foxhole in the cliff. 'C'mon,' he called, unhobbling the mule. 'We got to be moving on.'

Heavy drinking was by no means unusual in the south-western territories. Most men consumed liquor

140

frequently and copiously. The standard 'shot' in a saloon would be a quarter-pint-sized tumbler filled to the brim. At first Steve had been a 'happy drinker'. But as he gradually became mired in whiskey's fiery toils he noticed a change in himself: an urge to erupt into violence at the slightest spark to his keg. This generally occurred when he was called to subdue some saloon brawl: he would lay about him like a whirlwind, smashing chairs over men's heads. It generally had the desired effect. Men might jeer at him in his cups, when his speech was slurred or his hand unsteady, but they soon learned that they crossed him at their peril. Maybe the loss and lonesomeness, the separation from his son, put fire and hatred for the world into his fists?

These thoughts occupied him as he climbed slowly higher into these 3,000-feet or more high peaks along the border with Arizona, heading for Apache Pass. The air was clear, dry and heady and he could smell the sweet scent of the *piñon* and juniper. He looked around him at the mountain ranges, like purple cut-outs against the hazy blue sky, running away south into the distance that was Mexico. He breathed in deep, filling his lungs. It was good to be out in God's universe, away from the smoky saloons, the dusty towns. Yes, maybe he would, if he could, give the whiskey a break, try to start anew. But first he had a feeling he might have some killing to do.

The pleasant tinkling of sheep-bells apprised him of the presence of a flock on the mountainside, tended by a shepherd in a striped poncho. '*Hola*!' he called, beckoning him.

The *peon* appeared reluctant to descend, but finally did so, bounding down over the rocks.

'What you wan', meester?'

Steve tried him with border Spanish. 'You seen four *hombres*?'

The man nodded for reply. 'Yesterday. They cut throat of one of my lambs. When I ask for cash they pull guns on me. I cannot afford to lose a lamb.'

'That sounds like them. *Viciosos*.' The sheriff pulled back his leather coat to show his tin star. 'Killers. I go after them.'

'I would have cut their throats in the night, but what is the use? Then it would be me you chase.'

'They gone on up?'

'*Sí*, on up to the pass.' The herder unslung a goatskin bottle from his shoulder. 'Drink?'

Steve assumed it was water until he took a mouthful. It was fierce local *aguadiente*. 'Whoo!' he gasped, swallowing. 'Firewater.'

The Latino laughed as he was handed the liquor back and took a gulp, himself. 'Good?'

'Yep. Good. *Gracias*. But I'm s'posed to be sworn off the stuff.'

The sheepherder's dog had arrived to investigate Jock with some fearsome growls. When he peered up at the size of the wolfhound he quickly changed his mind and gave what could be called a sheepish flutter of his tail.

'Kill them for me,' the Mexican shouted, as Steve went on up the narrow trail.

When he reached the crest of the pass Steve looked down across Arizona Territory, or its south-western section. It was foreign country to him. In the distance was the adobe blockhouse and walls of Fort Bowie set amid a plain of grama grass. As he approached he could see it contained thirty rock and adobe buildings around the edges of a quadrangle of some fifteen acres. Its size surprised him somewhat. The Stars and Stripes was fluttering from a flag post, a bugle was calling, and soldiers appeared to be involved in military exercises with horses and cannon on the parade-ground.

Outside the walls some newer cabins had been built of pine logs. One of these was crudely marked in red paint: 'THE SOLDIER'S REST SALOON'. Steve eased the Peacemaker in his

greased holster, stepped down from
Moose, held his breath and quietly
approached. Although there were no
horses hitched maybe some of the rats
he was after were inside. He kicked in
the rickety door, pulling out his revolver
ready-cocked. When his eyes grew
accustomed to the gloom he saw the
place was deserted. The only rats were
kangaroo ones who scurried around the
shelves.

A man's raucous laughter made him
spin around. A soldier in the uniform of
a lieutenant was standing, hands
akimbo, watching him.

'You lookin' for someone?'

'Yeah, four varmints I'm after.' He
holstered the Peacemaker and gave a
grin of relief that the tension was over.
He showed his badge. 'I've followed
'em from Silver City.'

'You're way out of your jurisdiction,
ain't you?'

'No, they killed a cowboy near my
town. I can follow 'em to the ends of
the earth if I want to.'

'Well, they ain't here. They passed through five or six hours ago. Just paused to water their horses and buy tobacco.'

Steve looked up at the sun. It was already beginning its fall. 'Which way were they heading?'

The officer was a freckle-faced, red-headed young fellow, who smiled amiably.

'In the general direction of the San Carlos reservation. That makes me assume they would be headed for Camp Grant. That's where most of the riff-raff seem to congregate these days. They've built a veritable small township of saloons and whorehouses outside its walls to tempt our soldiers into sin and perdition.'

'You don't say? Yeah, I heard it was the hangout for horse-thieves and rustlers.'

'Yes, now the Apache has been subjugated they've been trying to set up here, but the captain ran them all out a few weeks ago. The men weren't too happy about it. This is a lonesome spot up here.'

'Must be a kinda unpopular posting.'

'Aw, it's not so bad. At least it's healthy, away from the flies and malaria down in the San Carlos valley. That's why they gave that bleak spot to the Apache.'

'You don't say?'

'Yes, I do say. Still, why don't you come in and have supper in the canteen? As you're on official business that would be in order. Be my guest.'

'That's mighty friendly of you, loo-tenant,' Steve drawled, gathering Moose's reins. 'Come on, Jock. Leave them rats alone.'

'Call me Red. Everybody else does. Discipline's a bit slack up here. Of course, I'd like to help you run these miscreants down, but we're not in the business of chasing civilians. We're just here to protect their worthless lives from the tribes.'

'Well, with Geronimo and his boys in jail it's all over, ain't it?'

'More or less. But occasionally we get a renegade bunch of young braves on the prowl, 'specially if they've been sold whiskey. That's the main reason the Cap ran the whiskey-dealers outa here.'

'You don't say?' Steve mused, as they strolled through the gates and past the soldiers on the barrack square. 'A few renegades about? I better watch my scalp.'

'Yes.' The lieutenant smiled at him. 'Yours and mine would be nicely to their taste — a yellow one and a red one.'

When he had eaten and supped coffee and been introduced to some of the men, Steve was urged by Red to stay the night.

'I got a spare cot in my cabin and a bottle of brandy we could split,' he prompted.

'No. It's tempting,' Steve mused, getting to his feet. 'But there's still a coupla hours of daylight left. I got time to make up.'

Red offered his hand. 'In that case,

Sheriff, all I can say is — good hunting.'

As he rode on his way down the steep gradient towards the San Carlos Steve called out to Jock, 'Waal, he was a pleasant young fella. Gave us a nice supper, didn't he?' It seemed a tad odd that he should have been so persistent with his friendship. 'I guess stuck out here he's just starved of conversation and companionship.' As he went on a bit further it occurred to him: 'Unless he's one of them funny fellas!' The lieutenant had had a rather limp and lingering handshake. 'Maybe I had a narrow escape.' For some reason this tickled him and he couldn't stop laughing. 'Or maybe I'm going loco?'

# 9

'They ain't gonna hang *me*.' The Kid knelt beside the supine body of Jimmy the cowboy. 'It weren't my fault.'

He swung on to his piebald and set off again along the river. He would head south-west and up towards Apache Pass. He would be an outlaw. He would rival the exploits of Billy Bonney. Hadn't he escaped from Silver City jail just like Bonney had (without going up the chimney). He would find Abel Crouch and his boys at Camp Grant. Arizona was ripe for crime. The Southern California railroad had arrived at Tucson and was heading on into Mexico. Now the Apache wars were over white folks were coming into the territory. There would be payrolls, banks, stage runs, suckers to be fleeced. He would form his own gang. He couldn't go wrong. He didn't need the

O. M. to tell him how to live his life. He would come back one day, his pockets filled with gold.

As the Kid climbed his horse up through the canyon he did not notice the men watching him, eagle-eyed, from the top of the huge rocks. The first he knew was the shadow of a rope, a wide-noosed lariat, falling down over him to pin his shoulders. And the next he knew was being jerked off his horse to hit the ground hard, the air knocked out of him. And then he was being hauled like a struggling puppet up into the air, his feet kicking.

'Well, just look at the fish we have caught!' Estevan's mocking voice made his blood run cold. The Mexican had ridden around the rock to inspect him. 'What shall we do with him, boys?'

Two of the boys in question were up on top of the big rock, having hauled the Kid high and wound the rawhide rope around a manzanita stump to hold him tight. They grinned down at

Estevan, one calling, 'Good throw, eh, boss?'

'*Sí*, good throw.' Estevan smiled and held his blue-eyed stallion steady. 'You will share in the reward.'

'What reward?' The Kid's voice was shrill. 'What damn reward you talking about?'

'The reward your family will pay for your safe return with all of your extremities intact. First we will start with an ear, and, if they don't pay, perhaps your nose. And, then, who knows?'

Others of his men had ridden up, his brother Emilio, taunting him.

'Why don't we kill him now?' Emilio asked.

'No, first he got to earn us some money.' Estevan smiled up at the Kid. 'I am afraid I have my boys to pay out on this, and there is the interest on my thousand dollars. So, it looks like it will have to be two thousand. Otherwise we hang you.'

'Two thousand?' The Kid gulped.

'The O.M. ain't gonna pay that. He'll be glad to get rid of me.'

'Maybe.' Estevan made a down-turned grimace. 'But I have heard you are a mama's boy. Maybe she will stump up for you?'

'No way, you greaser shit,' the Kid shouted.

They let him fall with a thump, knocking the wind out of his sails again. They put him on his piebald and took him away towards the Ramirez river, jumping down at a ruined rock-built house, once, long ago, the home of a rancher who had been burnt out by the Apaches. But one room was solid and habitable. The five *vaqueros* built a fire and boiled up coffee, laughing and joking at the Kid's predicament.

'What you gonna do to me?' he asked.

'Hey, why waste words? We better get on with it an' hang you,' Emilio said, matter-of-factly, putting his revolver to the Kid's head. 'You better step up on the chair.'

Kid Waterson did so, under protest, as they put a noose around his throat, slung the rope around a rafter and pulled it tight. He began to teeter on his boot-tips. 'No,' he croaked. 'Don't do this.'

'Look, he's pissing himself,' one of the *vaqueros* laughed. 'So much for the brave Americano.' He fired a pistol shot and splintered one of the chair legs to pieces. 'Ai-yee-yai! How you like that, gringo?'

'No, please, don't.' The Kid tried to balance on the remains of the chair that wobbled most unreassuringly. 'I'll do anything.'

'You theenk I can shoot the other legs out?' the *vaquero* sneered. 'You wan' take bet on it?'

Estevan, meanwhile, had a pen and bottle of ink and was scrawling a message on a piece of parchment. He leaned on the table and admired his handiwork. *My dear Mama — I am captured by bandits. They want 2,000 dollars for my release. Please pay, or they will kill me. I am frightened, mama. They torture me. They say they will hang me. They will send you bits of me. First you will receive my nose. Please do not inform anybody of this, not the Mexicans, not the lawmen, or it will be the worse for me.*

Estevan got up from the table. 'Let him down,' he ordered. 'Here, sign this. Add some words to it if you want.'

The Kid sat down at the table, gripped the pen, awkwardly, his hand shaking, and wrote: *Ma and Pa, please pay what they ask or they'll kill me. Your loving son, Caleb.*

Emilio took hold of one of his earlobes, sliced it off. Blood dripped on to the letter and the Kid howled.

'Here, send this with it. Thass just for starters. Next will be your cock, boy.'

★ ★ ★

It was a country of contrasts. Great chasms of rock swept down to dry stretches of virtual desert. The young

sheriff followed an almost impercep-
tible trail through a valley of ghostly
sagebrush and the foul smelling
*hediondilla* plants where the sun
scorched down and the heat reached
120 degrees on Gabriel Fahrenheit's
scale. Miles and miles were land
clothed with thorny cactus or
strangely shaped lumps of lava, where
man and beast were smothered in
clouds of dust.

At the junction of the Gila River and
the San Carlos he trotted past the thorn
fences and wickiups of what remained
of the Chiricahua Apaches after all
men of fighting age had been loaded
into rail wagons and transported East.
Their squaws, old men and youngsters,
stood in the dust and stared at him
as he passed, the surly hostility of
the defeated in their eyes. The benign
General Crook had wanted to give them
good land, teach them to farm and
raise cattle. But his successor, General
Miles, had crushed them mercilessly
and removed them to this region which

fairly reeked of the baleful malaria.

On Steve rode for many more miles through mountains clothed with sycamore and walnut, passing beneath the shade of great granite cliffs, and through canyons where limpid streams trickled. There was game in plenty, trout, antelope, peccaries, elk, quail in great numbers, herds of jack-rabbits, and he had a close encounter with a pack of seven bears, who, however, took to the woods when he fired a shot over their heads. He observed them all with curiosity, even the coyotes, eagles and occasional sighting of a puma, which other men would poison or shoot to protect their stock. Often he was led on his way by the swift-walking, long-tailed road-runner bird which seemed to love to give him a race.

'Hey, look at him go,' he yelled. 'Come on, Moose, you can catch him.'

The sides of the hazy blue mountains were often covered in dense forests of pine and scrub-oaks. Towards sundown, after several days of riding, he spotted the fires of Camp Grant on the flank of the Sierra Bonita or Mount Graham. Two years before few white men would have cared to make this journey alone and would have been relieved to glimpse the wooden-stockade walls of the fort. But it was the reverse for the sheriff, for when he saw the ramshackle array of stores and taverns that had been recently built outside the camp by opportunistic ruffians he smelt one thing — danger!

Cooking smells, *frijoles* and *tortillas*, from half-open Mexican dives, the sound of guitars and shrill girls' cries emanating from the beaded-curtain doorway of a saloon or bawdy-house, greeted him as he ambled in on Moose along the dusty street in the strange, ruddy afterglow of sunset. He glanced about him through narrowed eyes at the wandering soldiers on furlough, the Hispanic street-vendors, the honest traders unloading wagons, and the more-likely dishonest array of rough-looking *hombres* hung with guns who lounged on the sidewalk and watched him ride in. A fair sample, he thought, of the social driftwood drawn to the great south-west, some good, most no good.

He slipped down from his mule and allowed Moose and Jock to lap water from a trough before hitching them both to a rail and stepping up on to a low wooden sidewalk to enter what declared itself to be 'Hellman's Gambling Hall — whiskey and darnsin' gals a speshiallity.' It was a one-storey dive built of shiplap planks, lit by smoky whale-oil lamps which illuminated a scene of mild dissipation; men hung over a makeshift bar, or crowded around a roulette table. Loosely clad girls mingled among them, sweat runnelling down their chalked and rouged faces. Another 'angel of delight' in a dress of pink pinstripe, her blonde hair pinned high, a cigarette dangling from her painted lips, was dealing faro from a table adorned with the sign of the Bengal tiger. Others of the noisy crowd were involved in card-games of their own, their pungent tobacco canopy and stink of unwashed clothes adding to the prevailing fug.

'What can I do for you, mister?' A plump-breasted girl in a tight cotton blouse and short, scarlet skirt revealing her bare calves, was serving bar. Her face was frank and open beneath frizzy dyed hair. 'A bottle or a gal?'

Steve was going to automatically say, 'Whiskey', but he hesitated. After days of hard travelling without the juice he felt fit and clear-headed. Why spoil it? And, although the temptation to let the liquor flow through his veins and spin his head was like a strong river current inside him, he fought it and drawled, 'You got any of that sarsaparilla?'

'Sarsaparilla?' The girl's cheek dimpled. 'Sure, but it's the same price, dollar a throw. Amer'cun gal like me's 'nother dollar and upward dependin' on what you fancy.'

'I ain't lookin' to git a dose of Cupid's measles. Jest gimme the sarsaparilla. I got a thirst.'

'Sarsaparilla!' A lanky oaf, in a faded undervest and baggy pants suspended by string, standing beside him, spluttered into his drink. 'Listen to this milksop. He don't want to catch Cupid's measles! You still tied to your mammy's apron strings, sonny Jim?'

'Git lost,' Steve growled. 'I could drink if I wanted to. But I don't choose.'

He flipped the girl a dollar and smiled grimly at her as he turned his back on the loudmouth.

'You seen anything of a fella called Crouch?' he asked her. 'Bearded, wears a long duster coat over his suit, two fingers missing from his right hand.'

'Crouch?' She hurriedly shook her head, her eyes hardening. 'No, I don' know nobody.'

'Crouch?' The gangling drunk playfully tipped Steve's bullet-holed Capper & Capper over his nose. 'You wanna stay outa his way, sonny. He's a big bad man. He'll chaw you up and spit you out in bits.'

Steve straightened his hat patiently,

and sighed. 'Where is he?'

'Thass for me to know and you to find out.'

The sheriff's left arm flashed out, gripping the drunk by the scruff of his neck and smashing his head down on to the bar, pulling him up and crashing him back. The man slipped and staggered, blood trickling from a cut on his forehead.

'Where is he, I said?' Steve kept a firm grip on him. 'You want me to refresh your memory some more?'

'How the hell I know where he is?' the man wailed. 'What you hit me fer?'

'You were getting on my nerves.' Steve tossed him aside and shouted to the general company, 'I'm looking for a man goes under the name of Abel Crouch and his three sidekicks.'

A man at one of the card-tables called out, 'What you want him for?'

'We got business.' Steve had unpinned his sheriff's badge and slipped it in his pocket before entering the gambling hell. It might be best to remain incognito among such company. 'Anybody seen him around?'

'He's probably along at Willy's joint. It's a billiards-hall and cigar-store. You can't miss it. Or else they'll be out at Jake's cabin,' the card-player called, and turned back to his game.

'Good.' Steve shouldered the lanky oaf aside as a younger man hurriedly left the gambling-hall. No doubt an informant of Crouch. Forewarned would be forearmed. 'What the hell,' he growled as he stepped outside and saw the man disappearing into the darkness.

He loosened the Peacemaker in his holster and followed in the same direction. But just as he saw the sign: BILLIARDS, over a long wooden hut, three men rode out from the back of it, one in a duster coat and Stetson, firing wildly at him.

The sheriff rolled for cover beneath a wagon, pulling his Peacemaker and returning the leaden compliments. His bullets whistled around the heads of the desperadoes as they galloped away along the street.

Steve picked himself up and stared after them.

'They don't seem to want to know me. Or maybe they're planning to arrange a little reception party?'

He hurried back down the street. There was a clap of revolver-shot from the corner of a side-alley. A bullet smashed into a post by his head. He crouched and spun, firing at the flash of the explosion. There was a squeal of pain or alarm and the shadowy figure scrambled for cover. Steve ran after him and saw the silhouette of a man hobbling away down the alley as if he'd been shot in the leg.

'Halt!' he shouted and raised the Peacemaker to fire again, but whoever it was hopped away around the corner.

'Ain't got time to bother with you, buster,' the sheriff muttered. 'Must be the one who tipped 'em off. Damn backshooter!'

He got back to Moose and untied him.

'Come on, pal, your day ain't over yet.' He left Jock hitched to the rail, baying forlornly, as he swung on to the mule's back and rode away.

'Stay, boy, you come far enough today.'

He was worried about the hound's paws getting cut to pieces by the long, rough ride. They weren't as tough as Moose's hoofs. The mule brayed his anger at having to go on without supper, but Steve kicked his heels into his ribs and urged him on.

Out they rode from the rumbustious town-with-no-name that had grown like a preposterous carbuncle on the back-side of the army camp, out into the darkness and silence of the night, following a thin white dust-trail that wound away through the forest of trembling, white-plumed yucca, ghostly beneath the starry sky.

The dust kicked up by the fleeing gang of four was still hovering in clouds in the half-darkness and Steve could see by the light of the rising moon that they were not far in front of him. He was wary of a trap but the best plan was not to give them time to prepare it.

He went thudding along on the mule at a steady lope and eventually spied a solid log cabin at the entrance to a wooded canyon. There was a sheer cliff to the rear of it and Abel Crouch, or Herb Sontag, if it was him, had probably decided they could defend themselves better there than if they had stayed in the billiards-saloon. They, also, no doubt, had a good supply of ammunition inside to withstand a siege. Maybe they imagined he had a posse at his heels?

There was a tumbledown stable to one side where, he saw, as he hauled in the mule and jumped down, they had left their horses in a corral. He quickly tied Moose to a branch of a cotton-wood tree and flitted forward towards the cabin. He knelt behind the bole of another tree, raised his Winchester rifle and shouted out:

'All you in the house, I got warrants

for your arrest. Throw out your weapons and come on out.'

There was jeering laughter from an open window of the cabin and a shotgun was poked out.

'Who the hell are you?'

'I'm the sheriff of Silver City. I ain't taking no for an answer. I warn you boys, you resist under peril of death. I'm coming in shooting.'

'Clear off, scumbag.' A flash of fire from a barrel of the eight-gauge reinforced this reply and Steve flattened himself to the ground as lead pellets spattered through the leaves, cutting a branch toppling on to his head. This was promptly followed by the release of the second barrel.

'Howja like that, half-pint?'

The allusion to the sheriff's lean and compact five-feet seven-inches' height convinced Steve that it must be the tall and burly Abel Crouch speaking.

'That goose-gun don't frighten me none,' he shouted, raising his rifle and taking a bead on the window while the gunman would be reloading. 'Try this for size.' He squeezed the trigger and his heavy .44-60 slug crashed into the cabin's woodwork. He levered another slug into the breech . . . and another . . . and another, sending bullets whining and whistling at the cabin's windows. There were two other gunmen in there and they replied with similar viciousness as a full-scale battle ensued.

Steve ducked down, breathing hard, as the goose-gun joined in the affray again, scattering a wide arc of deadly lead, shredding the leaves above his head. It was too close for comfort.

In a lull in the proceedings he put the empty rifle aside and made a dash back towards the stables. But, as he got close, he caught sight of a man raising himself from the roof, carbine in his hands, and — in a split second as a shot crashed out — he rolled aside for safety. Steve came up, his elbows steadied on the sand before him, both hands gripping the guttapercha butt of his Colt .44, fired twice, and took out his assailant silhouetted by the moonlight.

'Aagh!' the man cried out as the bullet ploughed into his chest and toppled him off the rooftop.

The sheriff paused to make sure the bald-headed guy was dead, then went to find the mule.

'Well, they cain't say I ain't warned 'em,' he said to Moose as he took two sticks of dynamite from his saddle-bag.

'I'm giving you a last chance to surrender,' he yelled out, as he wriggled up through the sand and boulders to a position nearer to the cabin. This only instigated another fusillade of wild shooting that splintered the rocks and ricocheted, whining all about him. He kept his head down and calmly lit a fuse. He blew on it and waited for it to catch. He watched it fizzling, then hurled it overarm at the cabin.

'*KA-room!*' One of the walls collapsed and there were cries and shouts of dismay from within.

But, as he lit another fuse and waited for the dust to settle, he looked up and saw the big moustached figure of Crouch loom out of the open, shattered doorway, his shotgun in his hands, both barrels thundering their deadly load. Steve ducked for cover, then rose and tossed the stick through the doorway.

One hell of an explosion ripped through the cabin, a *Wouf!* of compressed air sending bricks, timbers, and bits of flesh and bones hurtling through the sky to rain down around the sheriff. Crouch was catapulted out like a cannonball and landed on his back a few paces away, bloody and dazed.

'Right,' Steve said, taking the shotgun from him and tossing it away. He clipped steel handcuffs on his wrists. 'You're nabbed.'

It wasn't an easy task piecing together the scattered remains of the other desperadoes — a severed arm, a boot with its mangled contents, a hat, watch and chain on a bloody torso beneath the rubble, this, that and the other — but he managed to establish that there were two of them and that they were past repair or resuscitation. Crouch was shaking his head, dazed, complaining of a ringing tone in his ears.

'I'm taking you back to Silver City. You'll get a fair trial, then we'll hang you. OK? On your feet, sunshine.'

'Git fugged, you . . . ' Abel Crouch let out a stream of obscenities. 'You'll never git me back.'

'You think so?' The sheriff hauled Crouch to his feet, a surge of violence from the battle still seething in him. He introduced the barrel of his Peacemaker into the bandit's loose, broken-toothed mouth. 'I'd sooner kill you now. I aint' foolin'. You want your brains spattered like your pals? Or you gonna git on your mustang and give me no grief? Which is it to be?'

Crouch tried to gobble a reply, his eyes bulging, nodding his head.

'I take it that means you see the sense of my argument. Right, let's go, shall we?'

He trailed Crouch, the dead black-smith, and their horses, on leading

171

reins back to Camp Grant and its adjoining whore-hole of a town. There was no sign of Jock as he went inside Hellman's gambling hell and bawdy-house.

'Hi,' the girl behind the bar called. 'You back? Yes, he's here. I've given him a plate of vittles. Nice dog, ain't he?'

'Yeah, like me, his bark's worse than his bite.'

'Really?' She smiled impishly at him, looking him over. 'I'm not sure I believe that. Did you find your friend?'

'Yeah. He's outside. I'm afraid his *compadres* are indisposed, unable to join us. They had a slight accident. Is there a lawman in this town?'

'You jokin'? You wan' another sarsaparilla?'

'No, I think I'll make it a whiskey this time. Just one glass. I've earned it.' Just one, he thought. Famous last words. He pondered the shimmering brown rotgut and tossed it back with a gulp, felt it shudder through him. 'No, just one. That's good enough. I gotta keep my

172

wits about me with this monkey.'

He tipped his hat to the girl. 'So long, nice to meet cha.' He ambled out, spurs clinking, as men stepped warily aside. He looked at Crouch sitting dejectedly on his horse, his wrists cuffed and tied to the saddle horn, his heels roped beneath its belly. He spoke to Jock.

'I think I'll book him into the guardhouse in the fort tonight. And then, boy, we got a long trail back. Still, it'll be nice to git home, won't it?'

# 10

Ranch hand Curly Gray was on guard duty leaning back on a chair propped against the log wall of the Watersons' ranch house, his carbine hung across his knees, when the hiss of an arrow startled him as it thudded into the front door.

'Jeez!' he yelped, jumping to his feet and peering into the early evening dusk. There was the thudding of horses' hoofs on hard ground and he saw a shadowy figure go galloping past the outer gateway of the ranch.

Curly opened the door and dived inside, slamming it and slipping the bolts home as the Waterson family looked up with surprise from their evening meal. Curly poked his carbine through the net curtain of the open window.

'Apache attack!'

'What in tarnation you talkin' about?' The O.M. wiped his mouth with his napkin and pushed his plate away, glowering at the cowboy. 'What flaming Apache?'

'Nearly parted my hair with an arrow. It's stuck in the door. Cain't see no movement out there but they's probably creepin' up on us.'

'Jed, go see what he's talkin' about.'

'Sure, Pa.' His eldest son unbolted and jerked open the door, glancing out. He stepped out on to the veranda at a crouch, his revolver at the ready, but all was quiet. He prised the arrow from the door and took it inside.

'Seems like somebody's sent us a message.'

'Hot damn,' Waterson growled, as he read it. 'They've got Caleb. They want two thousand dollars for his hide.'

'Who?' his wife screeched. 'Luis Ramirez?'

'No. He wouldn't stoop this low. It's his son, Estevan, behind this.' He reached out and took a sip of coffee as he studied the parchment that had been curled around the arrow shaft. 'Two thousand. Who they kiddin'? He ain't worth five hundred.'

'How can you say that? Your own son.' The big woman snatched the message from him. 'Let me see that.' She was not well-lettered and grunted as she struggled to read the words. 'Right, we'll see about this. What you sittin' there for, Jim? Sound the alarm, Curly. Issue the boys with rifles and ammunition, Jed. This is war. Your brother's life is at stake.'

'Hang on, Kathleen. Not so fast. I still give the orders in this house. We go in shootin' one thing's for sure, they'll hang him like they're threatening to. Yuk! Look at this blood. That's a bit of his ear. That's just for starters.'

'So, what you going to do, husband? Just sit here and wait for them to send his body back.'

'That no-good son of yourn got himself into this mess. Let him sweat a bit. I'll ride over and try to negotiate with Don Luis. Maybe he can talk some sense into Estevan.'

'For God's sake, man!' His wife was getting hysterical, waving the parchment around. 'This is an emergency. You go rouse the sheriff in Silver City, raise a posse. Us true Americans got to stick together, show these Mex they can't treat us like this.'

'Yeah, Pa. The Kid may be no damn good, but he is our blood. It's time for a showdown.'

'That's what that hot-blooded Estevan's trying to push us into. Why the devil did Caleb have to get involved in some drunken card-game? Why should I risk the lives of good men in a range war? I've seen one like this flare up over in the Tonto Basin. It spread like prairie fire. Before you knew it there were more than twenty men and boys lying dead.'

'Aw, don't talk such chicken-shit. All of a sudden the Kid's *my* son, is he? All right, if you're not going to try to save him it looks like it's down to me. I'll go in myself, and get the sheriff.'

'He's outa town, Ma. He's gone up through Apache Pass after Jimmy's killers.'

'Hell!' she screamed. 'I'll take a gun and go find these bastards myself, if I have to.'

'Calm down, Kathleen, fer Chrissakes. I've told you what we're going to do. Me and Harry will ride over first light to the Ramirez *hacienda*. I'll go tell Harry now.'

Jed tried to put his arm around his mother and placate her.

'Dad's right, Ma. We got to go careful on this.'

'Oh, you,' she sneered, 'sucking up to your father as usual. You allus hated Caleb. You don't care what happens to him.'

The young and fresh-faced Jed Waterson stared sorrowfully at her, shrugged his arms and started after his father. 'That's not true, Ma,' he called.

★ ★ ★

There wasn't much point in scraping up the bloody remains of the two men he had blown to atoms with dynamite. The ravens could enjoy a breakfast and their bones would soon be bleached white by the sun. He established from Herb Sontag, alias Abel Crouch, that their names were Ephraim Jones and Josh Smith.

'Obviously two of the Smith and Jones tribe,' the commandant at Camp Grant remarked when Sheriff McCormack reported their demise and hauled the dead man, Les More, in on the back of one of their spare horses. 'You can plant him outside the walls. We don't want him in here with our soldier-boys.'

Steve sold their horses, painstakingly pencilled income and expenses, facts and dates, into his notebook, and tucked it in his pocket. He paid one of the riff-raff to bury the former blacksmith and as he watched him dig fashioned a headboard, burning into it with a hot iron poker the epitaph:

Here lies Les More
Two slugs from a .44
No Les
No More.

He smiled wryly as he hammered it into the ground, then swung on to his mule.

'As for you, Sontag,' he said, 'don't get any ideas you can make a break from custody because I'd as soon put a bullet between your eyes as spit.'

'Aw, come on,' the burly, bearded man pleaded. 'Take these cuffs off, Sheriff. Look what they're doing to my wrists. You no need to worry about me. In fact, I'd just as soon be back in my cell in the Colorado penitentiary, what with winter coming on.'

'You got an appointment with a jury in Silver City. You'll be kicking clouds after that.'

'No, your duty's to return me to Colorado. They got first call on me. An' jest think of that five-hundred-dollar reward. I bet a sum like that ain't come your way very often or you wouldn't be just some hick sheriff.'

'Get lost. They can keep their five hundred. I ain't planning on hauling your butt all that way.'

'We'll see about that, Sheriff,' Sontag taunted. 'Soon as I get to Silver City I'm hiring me a top legal-eagle from Santa Fe. He'll tell you bastards what you can and cain't do.'

'It might be too late for you by then.'

'Yeah, and it might be too late for you, short-ass. We got a long way to go. You planning to stay awake every night to keep an eye on me?'

'I won't need to.'

Santag was almost twice Steve's weight, a coldblooded killer and as crafty as a 'coon. He knew he would have to be wary and keep his distance. Leaving Camp Grant with his prisoner he forced him to ride, his hands in irons, in front of him. The sheriff shot a jack-rabbit and roasted it on a spit when they made camp that first night. He threw a chunk over to the bandit, who sat hunched up, his piggy eyes watching him.

'One false move outa you and you're a dead man.'

Steve finished his coffee, tossed the dregs into the fire, and gave Sontag his canteen of lukewarm water to quench his thirst. 'That's enough,' he growled, snatching it back. 'Water's scarce.'

He got up and took the rawhide lariat from his saddle horn. He loosened the noose and suddenly spun it over Sontag's head, pulling it tight and hauling him off his log. He dragged the struggling man back to the bole of a cottonwood tree and roped him to it as he kicked and cursed. 'There,' he gasped. 'You won't be gittin' outa that 'til marnin'.'

'I'll kill you.' The older man raged, obscenely, until he realized he was hogtied. 'You . . . I'll have your badge. This is cruelty to a prisoner.'

'Tell that to the judge.' Steve settled down by the fire, wrapping his blanket around him, his Winchester between his knees. 'Jock, you hear him move you get him, boy. Goodnight, mister. Sweet dreams.'

* * *

Unaware of Estevan's troublemaking — he hadn't been seen for a couple of days and she guessed he was out on the range someplace — Madalena had persuaded her father to allow her to ride into Silver City, saying she needed to buy a new dress and other supplies. Don Luis had agreed on condition she was accompanied by two armed *vaqueros*. He did not like it, but, like her mother, his daughter was a very persistent and independent lady, scoffing at his fear for her safety.

Old Man Waterson and his foreman, Harry Hall, were, unknown to her, riding to confront Don Luis. But they would take a back route across the hills whereas she would follow the winding trail through the Burro Mountains to Silver City.

When her husband had gone, Ma

Waterson selected a shotgun from the rack, filled her coat pockets with cartridges, had her son, Jed, harness her buggy, and went outside.

'Where we going, Ma?'

'Into Silver City. If there ain't no sheriff to raise a posse I'll raise one myself. We're gonna scour these hills for your brother, thass what we goin' to do.'

'You think that's wise, Ma?' Jed reluctantly climbed on to his mustang and watched her haul her gross weight into the buggy. 'Hadn't we better wait for Pa to get back?'

'I ain't got time to wait for your father to go dithering around. My son's life's on the line.' She whipped the two-horse buggy forward, followed by a dozen of her husband's cowboys.

About high noon, Madalena Ramirez, in her stiffbrimmed hat and dove-grey riding-outfit, was about half-way to Silver City, sitting sidesaddle on her gelding. Suddenly shots were fired and she and the *vaqueros* spun their horses around with alarm as a horde of cowpunchers poured over the crest of a hill, fanning out to surround them.

'Don't shoot!' Madalena screamed, but it was too late. One of the *vaqueros*, Miguel, raised his carbine to return fire and was immediately shot from the saddle. The other, Federico, shouted to her. 'Come on! *Venga!* Let's go!' and slashed his quirt across the rump of her gelding, dashing forward alongside her, making a break back in the direction of the Ramirezes' land. His mustang was shot from under him and he went rolling into the dust.

Madalena whipped her gelding on, fear pounding within her, but there was no escape. Two whooping cowboys raced up alongside her, grabbing her reins, bringing her to a breathless halt.

'Leave me alone,' she cried at them, slashing her whip at one of them.

Curly Gray grinned, caught her arm and twisted the whip from her grip. 'No need for that, *señorita*. You better come quiet or it'll be the worse for you.'

'It surely will.' Kathleen Waterson had arrived on her buggy, trotting her horses up to them. 'Is this the Ramirez girl? Well, whadda ya know? Ain't she jest a lucky catch? Maybe we should cut off her ear right now like they done to poor Caleb and send it 'em?'

'What are you talking about?' Madalena stared at the bulky matriarch. 'What's the matter with you? Why are you attacking us? Is Miguel dead?'

'He sure don't look too healthy.' Ma Waterson glanced at the prone body of the *vaquero* back on the trail. 'He shouldn't have fired at us.'

'It was you came in shooting, you murderers.'

'Don't go calling us names, missy. Or you might be missing a few teeth.' Kathleen climbed in ungainly fashion from the light rig, grabbed hold of the girl's boot, twisted her ankle and hauled her from the gelding's back. As Madalena fell to the ground the older woman began pounding her with her fists and hefty forearms, screaming at her, 'What you done with my son, you bitch?'

Jed and Curly leaped from their mustangs and tried to haul her off, but Ma Waterson's blood was up. She snatched hold of Madalena's hair, swinging a piledriver to send her sprawling and sobbing into the dust.

'What's the matter with you? What have I done?'

'It ain't you. It's that damn brother of yours, Estevan. He's got my boy.' Mrs Waterson was breathing heavily as her son held her back. 'But now we got you, bitch. So, fair exchange is no robbery, dead or alive. But my boy, Caleb, he better be alive.'

The other *vaquero*, winded by the fall, had been pulled to his feet beside his dead horse, and Kathleen Waterson turned her attention to him.

'This bastard will know where they're keeping him.' She snatched Madalena's riding quirt from Curly and slashed the *vaquero* across his dark face, drawing blood as he recoiled. 'I'll whip it out of him and her, too.'

'We don't know anything about this.' Madalena was on her knees in the dust, her hair tangled, almost pulled from its roots, her dress torn and dusty, her face bruised. 'Neither of us does. Tell them, Jorge. You have no knowledge of where her son is, have you?'

'Oh, yeah,' Ma Waterson snarled. The man just stared mutely back at her as if accepting his fate. 'We'll see about that. Buggy wheels crushing his fingers will make him talk. And you, too, bitch.'

'Ma! stop!' Jed tried to hold her back as she slashed the quirt at the girl's back, cutting through the costume, making her cry out. 'We gotta get outa here fast. If you're planning on holding her we've got to hide her. We've got to keep her alive. Let's take her to the old mine.'

'How about him?' The irate woman pointed the whip at the *vaquero*. 'Let's thrash him. He'll talk.'

'No, Ma. I don't think he will. Hadn't we better send him back to the

Ramirezes with our demands?'

'Yeah?' She blinked at him. 'That's good thinking, Jed. You know, you got a durn sight more sense than that brother of yourn.'

# 11

Lightning flickered its tracery along the mountain ridges as black and viridian clouds rolled in from the north. Steve eyed them apprehensively. Most cowboys with any sense would look around for shelter, divest themselves of their gunbelts and spurs, their horses of their metal harness when a violent electric storm threatened. Steve had no wish — in fact, he had a natural human fear of being hit by a lightning bolt — no wish to go on in such weather, but he wanted to make up time.

'Ain't we gonna stop?' his prisoner howled.

'No.' The storm suddenly struck, crackling all around them, zigzagging streaks of electricity, balls of fire flashing in their eyes, hitting a cotton-wood tree, tearing it apart with a cracking sound. And then came the hot wind, whistling around them, blowing debris into their faces, everywhere, followed by a thunderous booming orchestration in the sky, shaking the earth, and the rains came down. A deluge of rain. All they could do was grit their teeth and try to keep the animals steady. 'Keep going,' he shouted, his words swept away.

It was not unusual. Since the millions of buffalo who once roamed the central plains had been all but exterminated by the white man strange things had been happening to the weather. For twenty years past they had been plagued by these summer downpours that set rivers racing, carved great canyons through the landscape where none had been before.

On the mule and horse they had been climbing up a goat-trail along the side of a ruddy red cliff and, as the downpour hit them with the force of rivets, the clay suddenly became water-logged and began to slide. Steve struggled to keep Moose up on the higher rock side of the trail. 'Come on, boy, hold it! Steady now!' he shouted. He could see that Sontag was in difficulties with his mustang and falling back alongside him, but it did not occur to him that the criminal would choose this moment . . .

All he saw was Sontag hurling himself from his saddle, his manacled arms outstretched to clutch at Steve's throat, and the next he knew he was tumbled into the mud and going head over heels down the slope of sliding ooze and shale. A rock jolted him to a halt and he felt the man's great bulk upon him. He tried to get a knee up to hurl him over, sought to claw at his eyes with his fingers, but it was impossible.

Sontag had his heavy knees upon his chest and shoulders and was pressing the chain of his handcuffs down across the lawman's throat. Steve kicked vainly as he felt his windpipe cracking, as he looked into the man's bearded face and crazy eyes, and knew he was being choked to death. There was another flash of lightning, illuminating vividly all around them for split seconds and he saw the terrified mustang go sliding by on the flow of water and mud. And then he saw the open jaws of his friend, Jock, as he sprang, landing on his attacker's shoulder, snarling and locking his fangs into Sontag's shoulder. It was the murderer's turn to howl with terror as he was dragged off the sheriff by the huge dog.

Steve staggered to his feet, choking for breath, trying to get a footing in the mud. He picked up a rock and slammed it into Sontag's jaw, and held it up to smash him again. But no, the big man was whimpering, holding his hands over his face, crying. 'Get him off!'

In spite of his predicament Steve could not help grinning at the burly outlaw's sudden change of spirit.

'All right, Jock,' he shouted. 'Leave him. Good boy.'

He fondled the wolfhound's head and pointed to the man. 'Guard! Good boy. Guard.' The dog gave an insistent growl as if he knew exactly what he had to do as Sontag tried to back away from his drooling jaws. 'I wouldn't tangle with him again or he'll go for your throat,' Steve warned him. 'Right, I'm climbing up to the top. I'll be back for you.'

It was as though somebody had turned the tap off up there. The downpour became a drizzle and ceased, the clouds rolling away as abruptly as they had appeared.

'Hell, what a mess,' he drawled as he looked at his mud-soaked clothes. Flood water was still rushing by and he could see the mustang had been washed way down the cliff side. But the mule had stolidly stood his ground and Steve began to climb back up to him. He had lost his Peacemaker in the fall but was relieved to find it just below the tracks. It took some time to wade back down to the mustang and haul him up.

'I cain't walk,' the bloody-faced, mud-covered Sontag wailed, as he lay cowering beneath the wolfhound.

'If you cain't walk I'm gonna have to drag you.' Steve threw his lariat-noose over the bandit's shoulders and fixed it under his arms. 'It's gonna be a bumpy ride, mister.'

'My leg's broke. I cain't put no pressure on it.'

'In that case I may as well shoot you. You're nothing but trouble, mister. Don't try anythang like that again or I will, I swear to you.'

He tied the rope to Moose's saddle horn and dragged Sontag up to the cliff. When he examined his left leg it looked as though he might be telling the truth — a bone was jutting out of the flesh below the knee.

'I oughta jest leave you for the wolves and pumas.'

'No. Don't do that.' Sontag grabbed at his cuff. 'Please, I won't be no more trouble. My jaw hurts. I think you broke that, too.'

'You deserve everything you got, mister. Don't blame me.' Steve took his

195

Bowie and went to slash down some boughs of pines from a clump on the mountainside. He roped them together and to the back of the mustang like a travois.

'Here,' he said, hauling Sontag onboard. 'You can ride in style like a damn Injun.'

\* \* \*

'So, you caught up with them?' the lieutenant called as Steve trailed in through the gates of Fort Bowie.

'Yep. Lost three of the varmints. Refused to surrender. Had to dish out some arbitrary justice. This one tried to escape in the storm. He claims he's broke his leg and jaw. Could your medic fix him up? I'd like to lodge him in your guard house overnight. I could do with some shut-eye.'

'You're welcome. Be my guest, Steve.' The frecklefaced lieutenant smiled at him. 'Like I said, I've got a spare cot in my quarters.'

'Humph.' The sheriff cleared his throat, uneasily. This boy Red was a bit too friendly. 'Well, that's mighty kind of you. First I gotta see to the mule and hoss. They're about tuckered out. We got caught in a mud flood.'

'Really?' The lieutenant eagerly followed him around, chattering in his affected East Coast way. 'They say these storms have come since the demise of the bison. The only good thing is the hordes of locusts seem to have disappeared, too. Strange, isn't it? Because, I mean, the buff' have been replaced by cattle. Take Arizona alone. In 'seventy there were only five thousand of them. Now there are more than a million. Surely that should fill the vacuum?'

Steve began to wonder if he had made the right move when Red invited him to take a hot tub in the officers' bath house, and insisted on perching beside him, gazing at his body, even offering to scrub his back.

'No, thass OK,' he demurred. 'Where's

that soap gawn?'

'It's down there!' Red dived his hand down between his legs. 'I think I can find it.'

'Don't bother.' Steve jumped up and hurriedly wrapped a towel around his private parts. 'I guess I got rid of most that mud.'

'You must let my batman wash your clothes for you. Eugh! Nasty aren't they?' Red held Steve's jeans and long johns between two fingers, tossing them into a corner. 'In the meantime I'll lend you a shirt and a pair of pants of mine.'

The sheriff was rapidly regretting his decision to stop off at Fort Bowie. It was good to be clean and to be fed, and, in fact, he enjoyed the young lieutenant's jaunty conversation ranging over all manner of topics, but, he figured, if he got fruity he would have to dissuade him by force, if necessary. He had an uneasy feeling that Red was making a play for him.

Still, it was pleasant sitting in his cabin in front of a log fire, as nights up in the mountains grew chill, and splitting a bottle of brandy. It was good to relax.

'I s'posed to be on the water wagon,' he drawled, 'but this stuff is too good to resist.'

'Why, you're not a temperance-committee man?'

'No, God forbid, but the whiskey around here's gotten its claws into me. It's dragging me down. You know, sometimes I've woke up of a Sunday marnin' sprawled on the sidewalk among the drunks thrown outa the Silver Garter, the ones I'm s'posed to have gone to arrest.'

'That's terrible. It's too humiliating for a man in your position,' Red mused. 'Yes, you must pull yourself around. My advice to you, Steve, is don't try to cut the booze out entirely. Just cut down. And cut out the moonshine rotgut. That'll kill any man. What you should do is order some good brandy like this and severely ration yourself to two or three a night.'

'What, bottles?'

'No, glasses, you lunatic.'

'Yeah, that seems like a good idea. Maybe I'll try that.'

'Yes, savour the aroma of this glass. Think of all the skill and love and work that's gone into it, made by people thousands of miles away for our enjoyment. Don't just toss it down your throat.'

'Yeah, I'll try. But it's very more-ish, ain't it?'

Red smiled and tipped him another glass. 'Yes, and I suppose a man needs a bottle in his hand, if he don't have a woman. Have you been married, Steve?'

'Yep. El Paso. Irene she was called. Led me a merry dance.'

'There's nothing worse than a crooked woman.'

'Aw, it weren't all her fault.' The sheriff stared into the crimson wood coals, remembering, an ache in him. 'I got a kid, too. A boy of six. I ain't seen him in a hell of a while.'

'I'm sorry about that, Steve. I was hoping to be married, myself. But there's not many girls would be willing to brave coming out to these desolate posts.'

'Even with the 'pache warriors gone?'

'They haven't gone. Not all of them. Didn't you hear? One of the Chiricahua scouts has gone missing. He killed a man who killed his father — natural vengeance according to their law — but now he's under threat of imprisonment by us he's gone on the rampage.'

'Who is he?'

'He's only young. He's just known as the Apache Kid. He's gathered a band of dispossessed savages around him. We've already had reports of *ranchos* burned, women raped, men and children tortured and disembowelled. He's gone on some kind of killing frenzy.'

'Whereabouts?'

'Who knows, he could be anywhere. Well, I got to turn in early 'cause reveille's at four a.m. We're taking a patrol down to the Mexican border. It'll be like looking for a needle in a haystack. He could be over in your corner of the territory.'

'Jeez, this ain't good news. I'd better be up at dawn, too, and head through Apache Pass. Thought I'd got enough on my plate with this packrat Abel Crouch, or Herb Sontag, or whatever he's damn well called.'

On this note, the two young men turned in, Steve dropping his borrowed pants and rolling into the cot.

'It's strange to sleep back under a roof,' he drawled.

'Yes, it is.' The lieutenant also undressed, lingering over his toilet, brushing his teeth at the bowl, before extinguishing the lantern. 'Tomorrow we'll all be out under the stars. Who knows what the day will bring? Possibly death? Possibly life?'

'Yeah,' Steve sighed, wondering what was going on back at Silver City. His body ached with exhaustion and the brandy had made him drowsy; he began to nod off. But, suddenly, in the firelight, he saw Red, palely naked, sitting on the edge of his bunk, looking down at him, enquiringly.

'Hey?' He tensed. 'What's going on?'

'A man gets awful scared and lonesome out in these parts.' The lieutenant put out a soft hand to touch the sheriff's chest. 'Can I come in with you?'

'Hell, no.' Steve gripped the young man's wrist. 'Not unless you want a broken arm.' And then he softened, meeting the youth's pleading eyes. 'Hey, come on, I ain't into that kinda thing. You got the wrong idea, Lieutenant. Maybe you better just get back in your own bunk. You could be court-martialled for this.'

Red hesitated, then slipped back across to his own cot. 'I'm sorry, Steve,' he said, a sob in his voice. 'I'm just looking for someone to be kind to me. It's so hard out here.'

'Go to sleep, kid,' Steve murmured. 'We got a busy day ahead. I understand how you feel, but it's not for me. We better just stay friends.'

In the morning he woke with a start to the bugle's call. Red had gone. The sheriff's clothes were washed, dried and ironed on a chair. He pulled his long johns on and went out on to the veranda. Through the mountain mist commands were being shouted, harness and sabres rattling, the gates being opened, the company of troopers wheeling out of them, the young, freckle-faced lieutenant at their head. Out into the mountains. Out into the unknown.

★ ★ ★

Don Luis Enrique Ramirez tossed his white mane of hair haughtily as he watched the rancher, James Waterson, swing on to his quarter horse, his foreman, Harry Hall, by his side.

'I will speak to Estevan about this.' He raised a forefinger at the departing Americanos who had come to protest at the abduction of the Kid. 'I have no knowledge of your son's whereabouts. But I will force him to give him up. He has gone too far. We must settle this, as you say, before the law is brought in.'

'Good,' Waterson replied, as he turned his restless horse about in the courtyard of the *hacienda*. 'I give you one day to return him alive and unharmed, otherwise I cannot be responsible . . . '

His words broke off as they heard a wild, screaming halloo from a horseman galloping towards them from the direction of the river. It was the *vaquero*, Jorge, who appeared to be as excited as his latheredup mustang. He reined in before them and shouted, 'They have killed Miguel. They have captured Madalena.'

'Who?' Don Luis demanded.

'Him.' Jorge pointed an accusing finger at Waterson. 'His men. His wife. She threatens to torture and kill her unless the Kid is returned.'

'You!' Don Luis stared at Waterson,

his hand reaching for the revolver in his crimson waist-sash. 'You come here to trick me.'

'I assure you,' the O.M. shouted, as his horse reared on its hind legs, 'I know nothing of this.'

'C'mon,' Harry roared, hauling out his own sixgun, 'Let's get outa here!'

He aimed his revolver at Don Luis, who was raising his own in Waterson's direction. He thumbed the hammer, but, as he did so, Jorge, incensed by what had occurred, unsheathed a razor-sharp machete and sliced it at the ramrodder's head.

Harry drew away from the whistling swipes of the weapon. He fired, point blank, and his bullet ploughed a hole through the *vaquero*'s chest. However, before he could make another move the *haciendado* swung his silver-enscrolled revolver upon him and his lead pierced Hall's heart, catapulting him from his mustang.

The gunfire made Waterson's quarter horse rear and plunge the more and, as he tried to control him, he stared with horror at his rugged ramrodder dead on the sand, at the revolver smoking in Luis's hand, at *vaqueros* running to see what the commotion was about.

He took the ramrodder's advice. He hauled his horse under control, then let him go, raking his sides with his spurs, as lead zinged about his ears. It was a fine horse, bred, as its name implied, for the fast quarter-mile race, and he sped away from the *hacienda*, his mane and tail streaking, his hoofs a blur, and was splashing through the river in no time.

However, one of his men had handed Don Luis his rifle and he had raised it to his shoulder, tracing carefully the course of the rancher before he squeezed the trigger . . .

Waterson was about to reach the far bank of the river when the bullet tore through his side. The impact almost toppled him from the saddle, but he fell forward around the horse's neck, and hung on.

'Go, boy, go!' he gasped out. 'We gotta get back.'

Don Luis prepared his rifle to fire again, but Waterson was weaving away through the clumps of longhorn cattle. It would be a difficult long shot and, on top of everything, he did not want to start a stampede.

'Shall we go after him?' one of his men called.

'No.' The *haciendado* raised his rifle. 'This is a bad business,' he murmured. 'I must decide what is best to do. First, I think, we must find Estevan before it is too late.'

★   ★   ★

The hills around Silver City were riddled with mines, most of which had, after decades of working, been played out and fallen into neglect. The one Ma Waterson had in mind was tucked away in a forgotten valley, its sides pocked with holes like Swiss cheese, great piles of spoil making the place a wasteland. It was used by the Watersons to store perishable goods in the cool underground away from the scorching sun.

The first cavern of this mine had been converted into rough living-quarters and some of the men often bunked there if they had to be away from the ranch checking the stock. Behind that was the barred and locked storeroom.

But it wasn't only tins of hardtack, barrels of corn, flour, or dried fruits that were kept there. Since the big slump that ruined so many cattlemen James Waterson had developed a miserly distrust of banks (and also the US taxman). Like many in those parts he preferred to get payment in gold coin. He was reluctant to stash his considerable fortune in his wooden ranch house which could easily go up in flames in an Apache or Mexican attack. So, he had taken to harbouring it secretly here at the mine in tin boxes marked 'Molasses' and 'Beans'. Even his wife was unaware of his true reason for fortifying this hideaway.

The heavily built Ma Waterson was sweating like a horse as she climbed her two-horse rig up the winding trail to the mine, followed by four of her more trusted cowboys. She had sent the others back to the ranch.

'You ain't gonna enjoy your stay here, gal, I can promise you that,' she sang out as she climbed down in her bulky skirts, and glanced at the bloody and dishevelled Madalena. 'But we ain't gonna kill ya, not yet, anyhow, if your daddy does as he's told. Savvy? So, git off that hoss and come inside.'

She waddled in front of them around the back of a wall of spoil and rocks that had been built up as a defensive bastion and entered the gloom of the mine. She lit a candle, slumped down on a chair by a table and filled a tumbler from a pitcher of cool water, slurping it down.

'Take a drink while you got a chance, gal, 'cause you ain't gonna be gittin' much else.'

Curly filled a glass for Madalena, which she accepted, sipping at it, her eyes in her bruised and swollen face solemnly watching them. 'You'll be OK, miss,' he humoured her.

'She won't be OK, that's the last thing she'll be,' Ma Waterson snapped. 'Don't go gittin' sweet on her, Curly, or you'll be out of my employ. Get that straight. You and Hank will take first watch 'til midnight. You other two will be on guard midnight to dawn. Then you take two-hour stints in twos after that. God help you if you let anyone near her.'

'Look, Ma,' Jed told her, 'I'll ride in to the Ramirez range under a flag of truce and offer our terms. What is it, a straight swap, the Kid for the girl now, no payment involved?'

'Thass right,' his mother said, wiping cold sweat from her temples and the grooves of her double chins, for it was chilly in the cavern. 'She must be worth two thousand dollars to them. Tell them that pays the Kid's debt.'

211

'Where shall we have the handover? And when?'

'Soon as possible. Soon as we know they've got Caleb safe we'll bring in the girl. Let's make the handover at the old hanging-tree five miles outa town. That way we stay in our territory. If there's any tricks we'll be ready for 'em.'

'That's good idea, Ma. Say high noon. Thass the best time.'

'Right, boy.' Mrs Waterson had found some biscuits and goat's cheese in a tin and was slicing herself a chunk. 'Say, this knife's real sharp, ain't it?' Her eyes gleamed maliciously, as she studied Madalena. 'Maybe we should send them the same token they sent us?'

'No, Ma,' Jed cried. 'She's had enough. That ain't a good idea.'

'Shut up, boy.' She had stuffed the cheese into her mouth and was gobbling at it as she lumbered to her feet, wiping the knife blade with her fingers. 'Hank! Curly! Get her arms. Hold her back. Pull her hair away from her right ear. Do as I say, damn you?

How you think they treated the Kid? It's an eye for an eye'

'No!' Madalena screamed and struggled as the woman loomed over her, her pudgy fingers caught hold of her earlobe and blood spurted as the knife cut her flesh. 'No!'

'Or an ear for an ear.' Ma Waterson's face split into a grin as the girl cowered away and she held up the dripping trophy. 'Here, Jed, take this with you. Wrap it in a bandanna. That'll make 'em think twice before crossing the Watersons.'

The cowhands and her son stared at the sobbing girl, their faces grim, before Curly said, 'Here, Jed, you better use this piece of white sheet as a flag 'fore them greasers start shootin' at ya. It's brave of you to volunteer, boy.'

'Aw, it's the least I could do for my brother. I'd better make tracks for the *hacienda*. Ma, don't hurt her no more. You've done enough.'

'Yeah, well you tell 'em.' She snatched at Madalena's nose, twisting it in her knuckles, making her squeal with pain, tapping at it with the knife. 'It's this they'll be getting next — a severed nose, like the 'pache do to their squaws when they been unfaithful. Get going, son. I'll see you back at the ranch.'

When Jed had gone and Curly had attempted to bandage the girl's ear to stanch the blood flow, Ma Waterson finished eating and drawled, 'Right, bring her with me. Bring your lariat.'

She took the lantern and led them along a dusty passage which gradually got lower and narrower. In the light thrown they saw ancient relics of mining, iron tubs, an abandoned boot, pickaxes, broken buckets, all with a desolate, ghostly look about them. Suddenly they came to a yawning gulf laid across which were couple of timber posts. In the light of the lamp they could see other support timbers and scaffolding criss-crossing down into the darkness.

Ma Waterson spat a gob of phlegm and tossed a pebble into the wide hole.

'Listen!' It was some seconds before they heard a faint pinging sound as the stone hit water far below. 'These excavations were made by the Spaniards. They go for miles.'

Her voice echoed in the silence as they stared at her, horror in Madalena's eyes as the woman took the lariat noose and eased it over her head and shoulders, jerking it tight under her arms.

'No, please don't,' the girl whimpered. 'There are rats and snakes down there. Let me stay up here. I won't try to get away.'

'Listen to the Mex bitch whine,' Ma Waterson smirked. 'Come on, Curly, lower her down. There's a cave about twenty feet down. She'll be OK, thass if she don't sleepwalk.'

Madalena crouched on the edge, petrified, as they tried to ease her over.

'Come on, girly, you gotta help yourself,' Curly insisted. 'Ease yourself down hand over hand, you can find footholds. I gotta take the strain on the rope now.'

'Come on, git going.' Ma Waterson pushed her hand into her face. 'Or you want to take the big drop right to the bottom? I can tell you nobody comes back from that.'

Madalena bit her swollen lip and tried to concentrate, deciding it was best to do as they instructed or she might never see daylight again. She guided herself down the dusty shaft as they lowered her, the rope cutting into her flesh beneath her breasts. She could hear their echoing whispers above her, like demons lowering her into hell, into a living grave. Her toes touched a solid lip of the pit edge and she swung herself into what seemed from the faint glimmer of light above to be a side cavern. She eased the lariat over her shoulders and it was whisked from her hands.

'No, please, I beg you,' she pleaded, 'don't leave me. I can't bear this darkness.'

There was mad-sounding laughter from above echoing through the caverns and the woman's voice came down to her.

'Don't worry, sweetie, you'll be all right. Just don't move around much, thassall. We'll be back tomorrow.'

There was a shuffling sound, the light disappeared, and they were gone. Madalena was left in the pitch blackness, the only sounds the dripping of water, the occasional creaking of rock against rock and of rotten beams. She cupped her hands to her head in terror.

'No . . . ' she screamed. 'No . . . '

# 12

The rains had made the flowers grow, swathing even desert stretches with carpets of colour, phloxes, marguerites, chrysanthemums, sumach, columbines, verbenas, and myriad others which Steve's limited knowledge of botany could not put names to. But he had little time to admire the landscape as he climbed through Apache Pass and ploughed down through shale and pines into New Mexico. He was in a hurry to get back. A prickling of the hair at the back of his neck warned him of danger. Something was going on.

'Aargh! Slow down!' Herb Sontag groaned with agony as his travois bounced and crashed, almost overturning, in places, the trail horse dragged along by Steve's sturdy mule. 'What's your hurry? Gawd! My leg! You're gonna kill me.'

'Maybe, with a little luck,' Steve shouted back. 'The sooner I git you in my jail the happier I'll be.'

★ ★ ★

James Waterson, too, was laid up, groaning with discomfort, sweating with fever, shock, and loss of blood after the Silver City doc had been called to try to patch up the hole in his side. It would be, most agreed, a miracle if he survived. The bad news was that Ma Waterson was now in command.

Her son, Jed, had made it home after a fraught confrontation with the mad-dened Ramirez clan. When a Mexican's pride was insulted then keep clear of the knives and bullets. And the kidnapping of Madalena was insult, indeed.

Most of the ranch hands were of the opinion that Jed, too, had been lucky to get back alive. None truly wanted a confrontation with their opposite num-bers on the other side of the Ramirez river, but when Ma Waterson went on the warpath she was worse than a frenzied sow protecting her brood. And the law of the West prescribed that in trouble no real man backed down from a battle. Much time was spent by the men in the oiling and checking of firearms, for word had been sent that Estevan Ramirez had agreed to produce Caleb Waterson to trade for his sister in two days' time.

★　★　★

Living in total darkness, unaware of how much time was passing, cowering in her cavern on the edge of the precarious underground shaft, Madalena, as can be imagined, was in a state of total dread. All she could do was pray, and sometimes it seemed that God had forsaken her. The feared prospect was of being abandoned in this hole until she starved to death. The woman was vicious enough to refuse to give her up. And Estevan, Ramon and

Emilio were only her half-brothers, born of Mexican women before her father had married her mother. She had always had the feeling they despised her for being the daughter of a hated Americano and what they sneeringly termed a half-caste. They were wild and proud and well might decide to kill the Kid. As a devout Catholic, it also worried her that, without final absolution, she was likely to die in a state of mortal sin.

★   ★   ★

Ma Waterson was not happy. Her mind, too, was in a tumult. She feared that the Ramirez tribe would try to double-cross her. What if the Kid was already dead? No, she would not produce her ace. She would hold that card back until she was certain the Kid was home safe. Accordingly, she left one 'puncher to protect her husband at the ranch, and told the rest to follow her to the mine. On the agreed morning she drove her rig at a fast clip out along the trail, ten of her cowboys, and several more men she had persuaded to join them from the town, loping along in her wake.

'You boys wait here,' she called, getting down when they reached the mine. 'I won't be long.' She went inside and found Curly, Hank, and the other two guards. 'How is she?'

'She's in a bad state, Miz Waterson,' Curly said. 'I lowered her a bottle of water and some biscuits li'l while ago. Shall I go bring her up?'

'No. Hank can stay here. The rest of you come with me.' Her rolls of fat trembled beneath her grey dress as she led them out to her posse, a loaded shotgun in one hand. 'Right, let's go.'

'Where's the girl, Ma?' Jed asked. 'You gotta bring her or they won't let us have Caleb.'

'Rubbish. They ain't having that greaser trollop 'til the Kid's safe back at home with us. I don't trust 'em.'

'But you said — '

'I changed my mind. It's a woman's progertive.'

The assorted ranch hands and townsmen glanced at each other sheepishly from beneath their widebrimmed hats. None cared to cross Ma Waterson. And perhaps she was right. You couldn't trust those greasers. They pulled up their bandannas against the cloud of dust kicked up by their horses and cantered away in a determined manner behind her buggy. It was nearly high noon.

★ ★ ★

The Ramirez men, Don Luis, Estevan, the now recuperated Ramon and Emilio, followed by a dozen heavily-armed *vaqueros*, rode their spirited mounts towards the rendezvous. They had, in their tall-crowned sombreros, and gaudy costumes, the air of picadors entering the arena to fight the bulls, arrogant and unafraid of danger. Or their pride made them appear so, for few men are unafraid of fast-impending death. Hard as life might be, few wish to abandon it in a hurry.

The Kid rode his piebald at their forefront, his wrists bound behind him, looking pale-faced and scared. When they reached the giant oak, known as the hanging-tree, for obvious reasons, in a rock-walled canyon outside town, they hauled in and lined up, cocking their weapons in readiness.

'Where they got to? What's keeping 'em,' the Kid asked, nervously.

Estevan slipped a noose over his head and tightened it around his throat, giving it a jerk.

'Hey,' the Kid whined, 'whadja doin'?'

For answer Estevan sent the rope spinning over the huge branch that hung over the trail and caught it as it came down. He tied the end tight to a spur of the oak's trunk so that the Kid was almost forced to stand in his stirrups. 'I don' trust the gringos,' he shouted. 'If they try any funny tricks your horse gets a slash on its hindquarters from me . . . and it's goodbye, Kid.'

The *vaqueros* murmured their agreement and Don Luis looked tense as he caught sight of a dust-cloud and the bunch of Americanos appearing from it led by the fat woman Señora Waterson, seated in her two-horse buggy.

'Where is she?' he asked, and, in a louder voice as they drew up fifty paces away, 'Where is my daughter? What have you done with her, you fiends?'

'You cut that rope offen that boy 'fore we talk,' Ma Waterson shouted. 'You harm him it'll be the worse for your gal.'

'No way,' Estevan shouted, angrily. 'The bargain is Madalena for this piece of filth.'

It was Curly who started the shooting, raising his Colt .45 and aiming at the rope above the Kid's head. It was the spark to a keg of gunpowder. Both sides backed away, whirling their terrified horses, firing indiscriminately, at the opposite line.

'No,' Don Luis shouted, his voice high pitched, but unheeded in the racket of gun explosions. 'No!' He raised his arms to call for calm and was pitched from his saddle as a wildly fired bullet seared into him.

Estevan did not hesitate. He slashed his woven quirt across the rump of the horse, sending it whinnying away, and Kid Waterson was jerked into space, his legs kicking, the rope's knot, expertly placed, jerking up his chin as it tightened around his throat to throttle him.

Ma Waterson did not hesitate, either. She whipped her horses mercilessly and sent them charging forward beneath the hanging-tree. She blasted the first barrel of her shotgun at the rope above her son's head, severing it, and he tumbled down into the buggy. She fired the second barrel at a *vaquero* who was trying to hold on to her horses' heads and sent him flying.

'Haagh!' she yelled and whipped her pair sprinting forward through the

Mexican ranks, hauling the rig around on two wheels, and heading back through the dust past her own ranks.

The flash of explosions, the roar of rifle fire, the whine and ricochet of innumerable bullets, was deafening as the Latinos and Anglos blazed away at each other, men of both sides dropping like ninepins.

Estevan shouted to his men to back off, to seek cover, but, as he did so, he jerked his arms back and his words ended in a croaking sound. Those who were watching him were horrified to see an arrow had passed clean through his throat.

More men began to fall as arrows hissed into the mêlée from both sides of the canyon's walls. They clutched vainly at greasewood arrows embedded in backs, in thighs, twisting around in agony and puzzlement for there was no sign of their assailants. A thin lance thudded into Curly Gray's chest, flattening him.

'Apache!' Emilio screamed, as he,

too, was tumbled into the dust, an arrow in his heart. It was the last word he spoke.

The men of both factions, Americans and Latinos, looked around them and began to back in together, closing ranks around the hanging-tree, kneeling, raising their carbines, firing at any movement along the canyon's wall.

'Where the hail they come from?' Frank Whiley muttered, as he reloaded. 'I thought they was all in the dungeons in Florida.'

Ramon, kneeling shoulder to shoulder with him, making war against his more ancient enemy, cried, 'Ai-yee! I got one.' He watched the Apache fall from the rocks and slither down the slope to lie still. 'The ugly bastard!'

\*   \*   \*

Steve McCormack pushed his mule as hard as he would go towards the sound of battle, dragging the trail horse and Sontag on his travois bouncing along

228

behind him. But when he reached the entrance to the canyon and witnessed the flashing and crashing of gunfire, the turmoil, men lying dead in pools of blood, others, wounded, trying to crawl into cover, he decided that discretion might be of more use in this situation than foolhardy valour.

He hauled the mule and Sontag in behind a large rock, took his rifle, slung his saddle-bags over his shoulder, and, followed by Jock, went leaping from rock to rock along the cliff-edge of the canyon. From there he had a bird's-eye view of operations. What remained of the Americans and Latinos amid their massacred colleagues had bunched together putting up a stout defence against the ring of encroaching Apache warriors. The latter appeared to be either older men or mere boys, those who had missed Nelson Miles's sweep to arrest all Chiricahuas of fighting age. They were darkly sunburned, almost black, starved and stunted, fighting with primitive bows, knives and lances, some with carbines. What they lacked in finesse they made up for with courage, closing in on the defenders, making almost suicidal rushes forward, several paying with the loss of their lives. It was clear that soon they would achieve victory and take vengeance on their hated oppressors.

Suddenly, as Steve watched, there was a scream from behind him and he swivelled around to see an Indian, his face tense with fury, leaping from a rock upon him. Steve swung his Winchester like a baseball bat, cracking his skull with the sound of a split coconut, and sent him rolling past him. He fired into him to make sure he was dead. Then he began shooting at others of the attacking party until his magazine was empty.

The Apaches gave howls of anger and one, who appeared to be their leader, a youth of dark hair and handsome looks, attired like a scout, doubtless the Apache Kid, pointed upwards and beckoned to his men to concentrate on the attacker at their rear.

Steve watched them as they raced off from the exhausted and ammunition-depleted men about the tree and began dodging through the rocks and scrub up towards him. He could see the gleam of hatred in their eyes and for moments he froze, turning cold at the thought of what they would do to him. He conquered his panic, and reached for the last stick of dynamite in his bag. He lit it as, in a bunch, they climbed closer and closer. He listened to the fizzle of the fuse and carefully tossed it at them. He ducked and listened to the roar of the explosion as dirt and rocks and blood and gore rained down upon him.

When he peered from his rock he saw that a good number of the warriors had been fatally injured. The leader — the Apache Kid — was hopping away from the scene, his leg blood-streaked. A few of the survivors of his band were hurrying with him, dodging from rock to rock, turning to fire as they went.

They had obviously decided that enough was enough. Today, the gods had decreed, was not going to be their day.

Steve, with Jock by his side, went leaping down to the survivors of the white men.

'What the hell started this?' he asked.

'I did,' Curly Gray gasped out, as he hung on to the lance in his chest. 'I shouldn't have, but . . . ' He began to fill the sheriff in on what had occurred.

'Where's Madalena now?'

'She's still in the mine. An' I think Miz Waterson's gone to finish her. She's crazy mad. You better hurry, Sheriff. An' you better watch out. She's got the Kid along.'

Steve didn't wait to hear more. He swung on to Estevan's blue-eyed stallion and, kicking in his heels, sent him speeding away out of the canyon towards the town, branching off along the trail that led to the Waterson mine. He gave the stallion his head, hanging low over him, and the brute galloped like a thing possessed, eating up the miles.

★   ★   ★

'What you going to do, Ma?' The Kid's voice came out like a croak; he was still dazed from the hanging. He watched his mother reloading both barrels of her shotgun. 'You gonna kill her?'

'Nobody hangs my son and gets away with it, 'specially not them greaser scum. Anyway, we let her live she gonna testify agin us.'

The Kid sat on a chair in the mine and leaned against the table for support. He watched his mother go hip-rolling away, a lantern raised in one hand, the shotgun in the other, along the tunnel. He clutched hold of the revolver she had given him and staggered after her. 'Hail, I gotta see this.'

What Ma Waterson had overlooked was the way voices carried through the mine which was riddled with ancient

233

passageways. Huddled, numb with cold and fear in her cavern, Madalena had heard the whispering voices echoing, 'You gonna kill her . . . you gonna kill her?' She saw the lantern-light splashing grotesque shadows of the huge, scrawny-haired woman and her scarecrow-like son.

'Oh, no,' she groaned.

'Missy.' Ma Waterson put on a sweetly syrupy voice. 'You can come out now. I'll throw a rope down. Step out on to the ledge where I can see you?'

'Oh no.' The girl huddled back further against the cave wall and waited, her heart pounding.

'What's the matter with you, sweetie? We're going to send you back to your family.' Ma Waterson tossed the end of the rope down. 'Here you are. Grab a hold of it, darlin'.' She suspended the lantern from a nail over the shaft, and thumbed both hammers of the shotgun, aiming downwards at the ledge of the cavern. 'Step out now.'

'What the hail's the matter with her,

Ma. You think she'd daid?'

'She soon will be,' his mother hissed, and, in more stentorian tones, ordered, 'Get your ass outa there, bitch, or you want me to send my son down there for you?'

In her frustration Ma Waterson loosed one of the barrels down the shaft at the cave entrance where she thought she could see the girl cowering. The explosion masked the sound of a brief gun-battle outside as Hank, winged by a .44 from the Peacemaker, quickly surrendered.

'This kidnap ain't my idea, Sheriff,' he whined. 'They're both along in the mine.'

Steve ran past him and along the tunnel as the shotgun explosion reverberated. Was he too late? The big woman was standing with her smoking gun aimed down the shaft and screaming abuse down at the girl.

'All right, hold it,' he rapped out. 'Drop that shotgun, Mrs Waterson.'

In her surprise, as she swung around,

recognized the sheriff, and blasted the second barrel at him, she stepped back, placing a foot on one of the rotten beams. There was a cracking sound and it snapped under her excessive weight. She screamed as she tumbled back into the shaft.

They listened as the scream echoed up to them for several seconds as her body bounced off the walls until far, far down, there was the splash of her fallen body and dislodged debris. Then silence.

'You bastard,' the Kid croaked out. 'Look what you done.' He aimed his revolver at Steve who flattened himself against the wall as he replied, fanning out four shots to the Kid's six. It was Kid Waterson's turn to scream, tumble, and go spinning down the shaft.

'Looks like he's gone to join his ma,' Steve whispered, as Hank joined them, and, below them, Madalena showed her anxious blood-streaked and dusty face. The sheriff shinned down the rope to join her, swinging on to the ledge.

'Come on, honey,' he said, 'tie this round you and Hank will haul you up. Don't worry, it's all over. You're safe now.'

When they both reached the top, he hugged her in his arms, and kissed her tear-streaked cheeks.

'Come on, let's get outa here. I bet you'll sure be glad to see the blue sky.'

'I surely will, Steve.' She forced a smile as she looked at him. 'It will be truly like heaven.'

As he escorted her along the tunnel and out to the excavated living-quarters of the mine there was an ominous rumbling sound behind them. The reverberation of the shots, or possibly the dislodgement of the mine shaft's beams, was causing a total cave-in. 'Run!' Steve shouted, dragging her with him. Rubble rained down at their heels. It was as if the whole mountain was quaking and rumbling. As they reached the outside world they were pursued by a huge cloud of dust.

'Wow!' Steve gave a whistle of awe. 'I

guess there ain't no point in lookin' for the Watersons' bodies now.'

He sat Madalena in the buggy, gave her his canteen of water to sip, as Jock, who had been outdistanced by the grey, came lolloping up, his tongue hanging out.

'Hey, give *him* some water,' Madalena laughed. 'He needs it as much as me.'

When the dust had settled and he had ascertained the girl was OK, Steve cautiously re-entered what remained of the mine. The living-quarters were intact but a wall of rock had half-demolished the locked storeroom, bending its bars as if they were putty. Steve stepped over them and struck a match. In its light he saw a glint of gold.

'Jeez,' he cried to Hank. 'Just look at this.' One of the tin boxes had broken open and spilled a heap of golden coins. 'Well, whadja know?'

He ran his fingers through the coins, picked up a double eagle, worth twenty dollars, and tested it with his teeth.

'Hey, look what Old Man Waterson's been salting away. A man could buy himself a nice li'l ranch with this.'

'Wouldn't that be dishonest, Sheriff?'

'Yeah, I guess it would.' Steve scratched his fair crop and considered this. 'But, as they say, to the victor the spoils. I think we've earned this. A man can't be honest all the time. Fill a sack, Hank. We'll leave him the rest.'

When he got outside he threw the heavy sack into the back of the buggy.

'What's that?' Madalena asked.

'Aw, just some gold that fall in there uncovered. We figure finders keepers, eh, Hank?'

'Gold? Who wants gold? Listen to that meadowlark singing. That's worth more than any gold to me.' She squeezed his arm and stared into his eyes, a sparkling blue the colour of the sky. 'And being with you. I never thought I could be so happy again.'

'Shucks, you're only saying that 'cause I'm rich,' he grinned and flicked the reins. 'Giddup. Let's head for town. You might as well bring that grey along, Hank. It's Ramirez property.'

'If Estevan is dead,' she suggested, 'why don't you keep it?'

'No, my ole mule's good enough for me.'

# 13

There was a letter waiting for him at the jailhouse from Hubert Gash, general provisions merchant, El Paso:

'That no-good ex-wife of yours has run off with a rodeo rider. Your boy is wild and troublesome. Unless you have any other proposals I will be forced to put him into an orphanage.'

It would be a long, hard journey: across the mountains to the Rio Grande, along the dreaded, waterless Jornada del Muerto to Mesilla in the deep south of New Mexico, and across the border into the northern corner of Texas to El Paso.

'The judge has decreed he can send for his mouthpiece in Santa Fe,' Steve told Epitacio Luna, jerking his thumb at the prisoner, Sontag, alias Crouch, behind the bars of the cell. 'I'll be away about two or three weeks. Don't start the hanging without me. And watch him like a hawk.'

'Don' worry, I won't make same mistake again,' Luna smiled, touching his bandaged head.

'One way or another things ain't turned out too badly,' Steve said to Jock as he rode the blue-eyed grey, with Moose on a leading rein. 'All we need now is to find a mate for you.'

Don Luis had made a good recovery from his shoulder injury and had insisted that Steve should have the feisty grey stallion for rescuing his daughter. James Waterson had survived, too, although he would never be the same man again. In some ways he seemed relieved to be rid of his ne'er-do-well son and unburdened of his wife. Steve had changed his mind about keeping the gold pieces and had returned all the cash he'd found to him.

'It ain't often you meet an honest lawman,' the O.M. had drawled and had rewarded him with a hundred dollars; Hank, too.

'Yep,' Steve sighed, 'it seems like honesty's the best policy even if I ain't never goin' to git rich.'

During the long ride across the barren wastes his mind drifted back to the day after they had buried all the dead from the massacre at Hanging Tree Canyon, when the lieutenant, Red, rode in at the head of his troopers.

'Yeah, trust the cavalry to turn up when it's all over!'

Apparently the Apache Kid had been wounded again when he raided another *rancho*.

'There's no sign of him,' Red told him. 'It's my belief he's crawled away into a cave to die.'

And, as time would tell, the last Apache warrior would never be heard of again. However, many, mostly Indians, believed he had found refuge in Mexico and lived on into old age.

'I want to thank you, Steve.' The lieutenant offered his hand before he led his troopers back to Fort Bowie. 'You straightened me out. I realize now out here a man's got to keep control of his feelings. This ain't the effete East. I should never . . . well, I'm gonna lead by example from here on.'

'That's good to hear, Red. I'd hate to see a nice young fella like you go to the dogs. I'm sure you'll find the right gal for you one of these days.'

As the lieutenant rode out he shook his head. He wasn't so sure. It was a strange world.

El Paso, when he reached there, wasn't the place he remembered. Civilization was fast taming the old West. True, there were still a hundred saloons and parlour-houses on Utah Street, open day and night, but there were churches, banks, a lumberyard, even horse-drawn streetcars. The streets might still be chuckhole sand but they were lined with posts strung with wires for telephones and electric lights.

He bedded down the grey and the mule in the livery for three dollars each and booked himself and Jock into the Orndorf Hotel. He looked out of his window at the bustle of carriages and horses and people down in the street and saw a gang of kids sitting on the sidewalk. And one tousle-haired one he suddenly recognized.

He hurried down the stairs to the street and made his way through the crowd. He called out, 'Jack!'

The boy looked up with hesitation and surprise, until he smiled. 'Dad? Is it really you?'

The boy ran to him and he picked him up and swung him in his arms. 'Sure it's me. You wanna ride with me out to the real West?'

'You mean it? You'll take me with you? You ain't gonna leave me?'

'No, Jack, I ain't goin' to leave you again.'

★   ★   ★

As was the custom the circuit judge, Dan Ramsey, would hold the trial in the Silver Garter saloon, there being no other suitable building available. So

Steve was having a beer with the girls before they got started and telling Groaning Joan about how the town council had awarded him a fifty-dollar bonus and a certificate of merit for that time he gunned down Sombrero Jack.

'What they didn't know was we were both so pie-eyed we couldn't have hit a buffalo at twenty paces. Jack had robbed the bank and was intent on making a come back and proving himself the equal of his dead protégé Billy the Kid. He was hurrahing the town shooting at everything in sight, staggering drunkenly around the streets. Me, I was so presoginated I could hardly raise my shooting-iron as we stalked each other, stopping for a snorter here and there. We blammed away to no avail. I musta used up two boxes of slugs. Finally, I caught him in the barn, crept up behind him as he was having a piss. 'Drop your weapon, Jack,' I told him. 'You ain't killed nobody yet and you only stole five hundred dollars. You'll only get a couple years.''

'What happened?' Honolulu Sal asked, stifling a yawn.

''Nobody's sending me to Yuma prison,' Jack roared, as he turned back to me and started shooting. He was only ten feet away so I was forced to reply. God's truth, I tried to get him in the leg, but I gutshot him. He died four days later, left me his watch, and swore he'd never been in a fairer fight.'

'Which goes to show,' Groaning Joan remarked, with a flirtatious smile, 'that God is on the side of the man with the best weapon in his hand.'

'Yeah, I guess.' Steve was not usually so loquacious on one beer, but perhaps he was nervous at conducting his prosecution case against Sontag's hot-shot lawyer who had arrived from Santa Fe. 'There he is now. Wish me luck, girls.'

'All rise for His Honour, Judge Ramsey.' The clerk banged his gavel. 'The case against Herbert Sontag to commence. Two counts of murder in the first degree . . . '

Sontag's lawyer, Hyram C. Schneir, he called himself, was a big man, with greasy hair, in a frockcoat, cross-over embroidered vest and loud-check pants. First he contended the jury were all biased against his client.

The judge swung a gallon jug of corn juice on to his shoulder, took a good swig and drawled, 'Why shouldn't they be? Who else we gonna get? Let's proceed, shall we?'

The sheriff decided to outline the basic facts about the killing of the cowhands, Jimmy and Roy, and leave it to the jury. But Schneir sneered:

'This evidence is purely hearsay. Will this person, the Kid, take the witness box to back you up?'

'Nope. He's dead.'

'So, all we have to go on is your word, the word of a man, who, from what I hear, is a legalized killer himself.'

'What do you mean?'

'You shot down my client's colleagues without giving them a chance to surrender.'

'Nope, they declined my offer, violently.'

'You blew up two of them with dynamite.'

'It was the easiest way.'

'I ask you, members of the jury, are you going to accept the word of this man? We have had no evidence from a coroner? No proof *in articulo mortis*.' The lawyer waved a document in his hand. 'I have here a writ of habeas corpus to show that Mr Sontag has been wrongfully imprisoned and shamefully abused since his arrest, as his injuries testify. It is the sheriff who should be on trial here. In all my many years practising at the bar I have never come across such a farrago of nonsense as that presented by Sheriff McCormack. Gentlemen of the jury, you must not hesitate to throw out these ridiculous charges. Otherwise, it could be contended, *in pari delicto* — '

'Yeah, well thass enough of the hocus pocus,' Judge Ramsey interrupted, mopping his brow. 'You jurymen got any questions you wanna ask?'

'Yes, Judge,' the foreman said. 'Why you hogging that whiskey? Ain't it time you passed it our way.'

'If it will assist your deliberations, by all means have a swig. If Mr Clerk will do the honours.'

The judge watched his clerk pass his jug around along the row of jurors who were sat on the saloon bar.

'So, what's your verdict? We ain't got all day.'

'Guilty of first degree murder on both counts and probably a lot of others, too, we don't know about,' replied the foreman, pausing from having a glug out of the jar. 'We're all in favour of stringing the varmint up. Those two cowboys were known to us. They wouldn't have hurt a fly.'

The judge banged his gavel. 'May I say I heartily agree with you, gentlemen. If ever a villain deserved to swing — '

250

'This is preposterous. I object,' Schneir shouted, as he pulled a six-gun from his carpetbag and tossed it to Sontag, producing a sawn-off 12-gauge for his own use. 'I've never lost a case and I ain't losing one now. Come on, Herb. The hosses are ready and waitin' out back.'

'Oh, no you don't,' the jury foreman yelled and hurled the whiskey jug at him.

'Oh, yes, I do.' Schneir blasted the first barrel at the row of jurors. As the pellets spread out in a twelve-foot deadly spray they all of one accord, like a row of puppets, dropped backwards off the bar.

Sontag, who had been freed of his irons at Schneir's insistence, was on his feet by the roulette table and aiming the Remington revolver at the judge, who took similar evasive action to that of his jurors, tumbling off his chair.

Everyone, including Steve, was at a loss because every man had hung his shooting-iron and gunbelt from hooks by the door when they entered the 'courtroom'.

'Looks like we gotcha with your pants down, don't it, Sheriff?' The bearded Sontag leered, turning the Remington on him. 'This is gonna be a pleasure.'

'Here, Steve.' Groaning Joan was standing by the door. She had slipped Steve's Peacemaker from its holster. 'Catch.'

'Oh, no you don't.' Herb Sontag turned and crashed out a bullet that splashed blood from her chest and made her collapse against the wall. 'You lousy whore.'

But the revolver had already been thrown, albeit not far enough. Madalena and young Jack were sitting at the back of the saloon, stunned by the turn of events. Jack darted forward and caught the Peacemaker as it arced through the air towards them.

'Here y'are, Dad,' he called, catching it, nimbly, and tossing it on.

Sontag crashed out a shot at the boy,

and spun to fire at the sheriff. Steve jumped forward to catch the gun as the bullet creased his blond crop. His left palm fanned the hammer twice, and the shots thudded into the big man, sending him sprawling across the floor. 'Thass from a half-pint,' he said.

The lawyer, Schneir, stood, taken aback by the shooting, an alarmed look on his face, but he raised his sawn-off to fire the second barrel.

'Oh, no you don't.' Steve beat him to the draw. The lawyer tumbled back to the floor, a neat red hole between his eyes.

'Great shooting, Dad. You did it.' The boy ran up and hugged Steve. 'Hey, watch out!' He pointed at Sontag who was raising his revolver from the floor for a last shot. The sheriff turned and finished him with his final two bullets.

The jurors and the judge peered through the rolling gunsmoke from their hiding places as Steve told his son:

'Nobody likes killin' a man but somebody's got to exterminate these vermin.'

He went over to Groaning Joan who was lying on the boards bleeding profusely from her chest wound. He knelt beside her, holding her hand.

'Thanks, Joan. You're gonna be OK.'

'No, I'm going fast, Steve. Promise me one thing. Give me a good send-off and a headstone. I don't' wanna be forgot.'

'You'll get the best, Joan. A hearse with two black horses, ostrich feathers on their heads. A corner plot in the shade of the cottonwood an' I'll plant anemones on your grave.'

Groaning Joan smiled, clutched at Madalena's hand. 'Be happy together. You've got a good man.' She groaned for the last time as the life passed out of her.

Steve wiped tears from his eyes and closed hers, then stood and drawled, 'I reckon the case is closed, Judge.'

'I reckon it is.' Judge Ramsey picked up the fallen whiskey jar. 'You done a good job. One rarely sees a case brought to such a satisfactory conclusion. Have a drink.'

'Just one shot.' Steve tipped the jug

to his mouth and grinned. 'Well, maybe two. That's all I'm having from here on.'

'Two shots for the sheriff,' the judge said. 'Anybody else got a thirst?'

'Remember Groaning Joan,' the sheriff mused, looking down at her. 'A heroine who saved the town.'

Loved by all.
Today Joan sleeps alone.

He scratched his head and grinned as he led them outside into the sunshine. 'Or somethang like that. I'll work on it. Hey, you know that hundred dollars the O.M. gave me? I've bought a nice li'l cottage up the street a bit.' He put on arm around Madalena's waist and the other around his son's shoulders. 'Let's go take a look. I reckon it'll make us a fine home. I cain't expect y'all to live in the jailhouse.'

# RODEO RENEGADE

## Ty Kirwan

When English couple Rufus and Nancy Medford inherit a ranch in New Mexico, they find the majority of their neighbours are hostile to strangers. Befriended by only one rancher, and plagued by rustlers, the thought of returning to England is tempting, but needing to prove himself, Rufus is coached as a fighter by a circus sharp shooter, the mysterious Ghost of the Cimarron. But will this be enough to overcome the frightening odds against him?